PROPERTY OF DREX #1

DEATH CHASERS MC SERIES

C.M. Owens

Acknowledgements

Cover model: **Derrick Keith Shane Meacham**

Photographer: **Eric Battershell Photography**

Cover Designer: **Book Cover By Design**

ISBN-13:
978-1532976605

The worst decisions are made by the desperate or the foolish...

Chapter 1

EVE

"*Y*ou should strip. These clothes aren't going to cut it. And I also need to search you. Everywhere."

He removes his hand and steps away, watching and waiting, and I swallow hard. The painful knot in my throat only grows as I reach for the hem of my shirt. Taking a deep breath, I pull it off quickly.

His eyes are on me, watching with open interest as I move to my jeans. As much as I'd like to draw this out and delay the inevitable, I also don't want to keep dreading the first time. The sooner I'm naked, the sooner the suspense ends. I've prepared myself for what I hope is the worst.

"You know what's going to happen to you, right?" he asks, crossing his arms over his chest as I push the jeans down my legs.

He takes a deep breath as I step out of them.

In nothing but my pink, cotton underwear, I try to find the courage to meet his gaze, keeping my expression as impassive as possible under the grim circumstances.

"I know."

1

Chapter 2

EVE

Two Days Ago...

"So you came to me because you need money. For your family," Benny says, stroking his beard as he eyes me. It's not a question; he's just laying the facts out there, summarizing.

Swallowing back my nerves, I chance a glance at Ben, my best friend since grade school. When he suggested asking his dad for help, I wasn't planning on it being this intimidating. Then again, I should have.

Walking into the clubhouse for the Hell Breathers motorcycle club—one of the biggest around—should have reminded me how stupid this is. But desperate and stupid go hand in hand, it seems.

"Yes, sir. My dad left behind a huge—"

"The details aren't necessary," Benny interrupts, his creepy grin spreading as his eyes roam over me, appraising me in a way that leaves me feeling like I need a shower. "All that matters is that you know what will be expected of you. You'll do anything asked. As a somewhat intelligent girl, I'm sure you can figure out the consequences if you try to change your mind."

Some of the other bikers step up, smirking for the most part. Several lick their lips suggestively, warning me of what's to come. This isn't what I had in mind, and now I wish I'd worn a sweatshirt to hide me better, even though it's hot as hell outside.

"Dad, you can't—" Ben's words are cut off when he's slapped down to the ground.

It all happens so fast that the action doesn't even have time to register in my mind until it's over. I want to look down to see if he's okay, but I'm too scared to take my eyes off Benny now.

"You know better," Benny says, talking to his son, but keeping his eyes locked on me. "I don't give away money for free. If Eve wants it, she'll have to agree to the terms."

A wave of nausea slams into me, making it impossible to stand here without turning pale, or maybe I'm turning puce. I should have expected this when he told me to bring proof of a clean bill of health, yet I was naïve enough to believe Ben's father would see me as a child instead of a woman.

"Think about it, Eve," Benny says, turning his back on me as he faces his menacing crew. "You have two days to decide what to do. If you say yes, remember how permanent it is. Once you're in, you're always in. If you say no, then... well, good luck."

With that, he and his guys walk off, leaving me at the entryway with a bleeding Ben. He wipes his mouth with the back of his hand,

3

regret and anger shading his eyes.

"I'm sorry, Eve. I didn't know he'd do this. I swear I thought he'd just give you the money."

My lips tighten into a thin line. I forgot a very important fact in life; you never get something for free.

The depths of depravity I would have to face isn't worth it. Not with a man who I grew up knowing as my best friend's father. It's just sick.

"Come on. I'll get you out of here," Ben says apologetically. "We'll figure something else out. I have a little money saved up. It's nowhere near enough, but it might help you until you can get more."

I have to figure something else out, because this is no longer an option.

Chapter 3

EVE

"Ben called to talk to you. Says he can't reach you on your phone," Mom says softly as she comes out of the twins' room.

Moving past her, I peek in to see both of my five-year-old brothers sleeping peacefully in their separate beds. One more day before Benny The Sicko shuts the door on his disgusting offer. But I don't know how else I can get that sort of money.

I walk in and kiss both of my younger brothers, smiling when Joshua sighs happily in his sleep. In that moment, I start questioning all the possibilities. If I don't find the money, Mom will be broke and homeless within a week. The bank will repossess the house. Her wages will be garnished to pay the hospital bills she can't afford. And the twins could end up in foster care if she loses the ability to care for them.

Even with welfare, she won't be able to dig out of this hole, thanks to my stupid, selfish, piece of shit, suicidal father. How could he take the easy way out and leave all of his secret burdens on my mother?

Mom's still recovering from the car accident they were in over two years ago. She's had to have numerous surgeries over the course of those two years on the leg that was shattered, only driving up the hospital bills that much more. Her leg is healing slowly from the most recent one, and she's still limping.

"They took the car today?" I ask, frowning as I walk into the kitchen. I've kept quiet in front of the boys. They're too young to hear this stuff.

"Yeah," she says sadly, her strength wavering in front of my eyes.

She's tried so hard to be strong since Dad ended his troubles with a bottle of pills, but someone can only take so much before breaking.

"I'm sorry, sweetie," she says, covering her face in shame when she can't hold back her tears.

I quickly go to sit down beside her, wishing I could come up with anything to offer her peace. Wrapping my arms around her, I pull her close, feeling the knot in my throat double in size.

"What about my tuition money? Did the school call back yet?"

We can get that money back and use it toward bills instead of school. It won't be nearly enough, but it could buy us some more time. Maybe. If the bank and hospital would work with us—

Her bitter laughter that cuts through my thoughts doesn't hold much promise, and I frown before she even has to confirm my dread.

"Your dad never paid the new year's tuition. I... I can't believe he did this."

Watching my mother fall apart at our dining room table while the dishes lay spread out in front of me, depleted of food we can't afford because she has three children that need her, I decide what I have to do. This will save their lives even if it destroys mine.

Mom doesn't have to know where the money is from. She doesn't have to learn about the sacrifice I'm making. I'll see her when I can, and lie to her the rest of the time.

Walking away from her, I pull out my phone. Ben has tried calling at least a hundred times, but I'm finally ready to talk.

Chapter 4

EVE

"Don't do this," Ben whisper-scolds, pleading with me as he follows close behind.

He spent the night trying to talk me out of this, even refused to call his father. That put the burden of talking to the devil on my shoulders, but I did it. I called hell, Satan answered, and I sold my soul for my family's security in less than ten minutes.

My steps don't even slow as I make my way toward a smiling Benny. Ignoring the protest of my roiling stomach, I silently accept my fate. Then I turn to look at the sad eyes on the boy who doesn't want to see me turn myself over to the hands of Hell's king.

I have no idea when—or *if*—I'll get to see my family, or how often.

"It's okay, Ben," I say to comfort him.

"Please, Eve. Don't."

I smile grimly as I turn away from him, ignoring the bite of anger in his tone. The only boy to ever have had me in his bed is being forced to turn me over to his twisted father to do things that will destroy me. Obviously he's mad at me for my decision, but *it is* my decision.

Taking a shaky breath, I face Benny, bringing myself as close as my feet will allow. Standing at least two feet away, Benny nods, smiling as though I'm the prey that just came willingly into his jaws.

"Very nice, Eve. Although I wish you had worn something... sexier."

He throws a leg over his massive black beast of a bike, and tosses me a helmet that falls to my feet when my arms refuse to move. I stare down my jean-clad legs to my sandaled feet where the helmet rests beside.

"Put it on. Drex is waiting."

Who?

Ben gasps behind me, and I turn to see his ashen face. With his mouth hanging that way and pure horror in his eyes, I'm assuming this is even worse than I thought.

"You're taking her to the Death Dealers?" Ben asks in a hushed whisper reserved for blasphemy. "You know you can't do that. Her fath—"

"Yeah. I can do it," Benny interrupts. "Time to offer up some peace. They've been toying with me about something, and I want the

9

info they have. Drex is taking her to his father. I'm sure Herrin is going to love her. It's not too often sweet ones like this march their pretty little asses into the clubhouse and offer up their bodies."

My knees wobble, but I don't fall, thankfully. Death Dealers? Drex isn't a name I've heard, but Death Dealers definitely are a name I've heard. That's even worse than Hell Breathers.

"Get your ass in gear, sugar. Drex isn't patient," Benny prompts.

Unsteady and trembling, I reach down for the helmet, ignoring the guys who grab my bags from Ben's hands.

The Death Dealers have a reputation… Ruthless. Depraved. Dirty. Most importantly, brutal. I'm really hoping it's all just been hearsay stuff that doesn't hold any real truth. Everything sounds worse than it actually is, right?

I'm not sure how many girls offer themselves up, but I have a feeling I'm going to be just as regretful as the ones who do.

Bearded men who barely groom whistle at me as I make my way to Benny and his bike. They all put on their helmets and sunglasses, looking just as scary as demons on wheels.

"Hop on," Benny says while making the beast between his legs roar to life, and startling me enough to jump.

His taunting laughter is barely heard over the bike's vicious engine. Maybe I'll get lucky and Drex's father won't find me to be his type, therefore letting me go.

Dreams are just for the foolish who refuse to accept reality. Especially when their reality just turned as dark as mine.

Chapter 5

EVE

Benny kills the engine just as we reach an old warehouse, one that seems to have been abandoned long ago. But there's no sign of any other bikers.

"Your mom should have received the money by now. You can call her if you want, but make it brief."

I decide to send a text instead, considering my voice seems to have run away with the logical half of my mind.

Me: *I'm going away for a while. Sorry about leaving you like this, but I got a job in LA. I'll call when I can.*

I'm still in Texas—closer to the Mexican border than I was—but I'm far enough away from home that Mom won't accidentally run into me. That is... if I even get to leave. I shudder just thinking about being turned into a sex slave.

Almost immediately, my phone buzzes with a text.

Mom: *Don't play games. You're not going to believe what just happened, but we don't have to worry about money right now. Hurry home so I can explain better.*

A small tear escapes my eye, reminding me this is all worth it. My family is taken care of. That's all that really matters. I'm just collateral damage in the grand scheme of things.

"Don't go back on your word," Benny warns, his lips twitching in sadistic amusement as he stands and looks at me.

Clumsily, I clamber off the bike, pulling the helmet off without grace. I feel my hair wildly tousled around my head, but I don't fix it. I'd rather be as unappealing as possible right now.

"I have no intentions of going back on my word," I say through emotional strain.

His dark grin emerges, giving me a peek at the true devil beneath the flesh.

"Good. I'd hate to carve up that pretty little face."

Chapter 6

DREX

"They're at the warehouse, and they have a girl, just like they promised," Sledge says, looking at me before he resumes his place on his bike.

I glance toward the road, still leery of this supposed *peace* offering.

"Not sure why we need them to give us a girl. They'd pour in off the streets if we opened our doors," I tell him, pissed off by this whole *exchange*.

This is all too shady and bizarre. A fucking girl being presented as currency? We've sure as hell never done anything like this before, and I don't trust a damn thing Benny Highland does.

"We don't deal in human trafficking," I remind Sledge when he doesn't say anything. "And that's exactly what this sounds like."

Sledge grunts something in agreement, but Axle speaks as he walks up to us.

"Supposedly this is all consensual. No trafficking involved. Why are we doing this? Beats the fuck outta me. It all sounds a little suspicious."

I abso-fucking-lutely agree with him on that last part. It's suspicious as hell, and I don't see the point in doing this shit.

"Herrin just wants to see what they're up to. More than likely she's a spy that Benny and his guys want to insert into our crew. Benny has never had enough finesse to do something on the discreet side. Herrin wants to have some *fun* getting the truth out of her," Sledge says, smirking.

I nod, even though I'm still not sold on this idea. But Pop is the P. Not me. His word is final.

"And if she's not a spy?" I ask Sledge.

"Then your dad gets a new toy that hasn't been jaded by our world. Benny's claiming the girl is as sweet and golden as anything he's ever seen."

"Virgin?" I ask, laughing hysterically.

Dad will destroy a girl that innocent.

"No, but not far from a virgin." Sledge grins as he finishes the statement, seeming as amused as I am.

I shake my head, pitying the fool girl going through with this. She'll be nothing more than a corpse if she's working with Benny.

"I think you should stay here and let us check this out." Sledge surprises me with his abrupt shift in conversation.

I just arch a brow at him. If he thinks I'm scared of a worm like Benny, he's lost his mind.

"If I don't show up, it'll look like I'm afraid of him. Just have our guys ready to take them out from the rooftops if it looks like they're luring us into a trap."

"It won't look weak," he murmurs while putting his glasses back on. "Your father isn't coming because he's smart."

"Pop has a bigger target on his back than I do. He killed Benny's brother five years ago. If Benny wants a shot at me, he's dumber than he looks. Pop would gut him and make sure he got to watch his own intestines being pulled from his body."

Sledge smiles fondly of that imagery, then he starts up his engine, making it purr. "You're the boss. We'll do it your way."

I nod and start my bike back up, ready to get this over with. Everyone follows my lead. Sledge stays close to my right, keeping his front wheel next to my back one. Hershel—Pop's second longest loyalist—takes my left, getting even with Sledge.

We pace ourselves, crawling into the warehouse parking lot like we have all the time in the world. Between the abandoned containers and rusted, forgotten objects littering the otherwise vacant lot, our engines echo and resound, making it sound as though we're hundreds instead of twenty.

Just as we round the corner of the old warehouse, we see the relaxed crew of the Hell Breathers. They're all propped against their bikes or leisurely sitting on them, waiting for us as though it's been hours instead of ten minutes.

Sledge and Hershel both ride up beside me, putting their bikes even with mine as they warily keep an eye on Benny and his men. Benny's son isn't here. Probably for the best. Boy doesn't have the black heart for this business. Or the iron stomach.

But usually Benny brings him along, trying to groom him for his place in the business. It's suspicious that he didn't tag along this time, and I scan the scene warily.

After coasting to a stop, I kill my bike, letting quietness descend when my guys follow suit. Benny smirks, which immediately has me discreetly tensing, but my tension eases quickly because he's too relaxed to have anything up his sleeve.

I prop up on my handlebars, looking around but not seeing this *girl* they've brought.

"Where's this big peace offering?" I ask, feigning a yawn.

He looks toward one of his guys and gives him a nod, which then prompts the guy to head toward the warehouse doors.

"This means no more of your men showing up on my streets and

17

causing a scene. You know that, right?"

It's my turn to smirk.

"Pop tell you that?" I drawl, amused.

Benny narrows his eyes at me, doing his best to be intimidating. We've been ruining their "fear" factor lately, showing people what pussies they really are.

"He said he'd let you determine if she was worth the peace. Personally, I'd think you'd enjoy not looking over your shoulder every time you go to get something to eat."

My smirk turns into an entertained grin. They usually stay at least three towns over, but in the past year and a half, they've encroached on our space in Halo.

"Haven't been looking over my shoulder, Benny," I lie, because we all look over our shoulders, but not just because of him.

His jaw grinds for a second as he cracks his neck to the side. "It's rare a gem like this falls into our laps. Most of our girls are hardened like us. Nothing wrong with that, but this is a new flavor, and she's his for the taking. Usually getting a girl like this requires force."

I tense at that. That's one thing I don't allow in my crew. Pop doesn't mind it, but it's pretty fucking disgusting to me. If they're giving it away, I'll take it. I don't have to force myself. Shitheads like Benny probably don't have a choice.

18

"I'm not sure one girl is enough to ice the bad blood between us," I say, shrugging while acting bored with all of this.

"It's just a symbol, Drex. This is me taking the first step to put our bad blood to rest. If we're constantly at war, then someone else will eventually take advantage of us once we've weakened each other. Herrin agrees. Which is why you're supposed to turn over some information to me as a show of your peace offering."

That's the real reason he's giving us this girl. He wants to know which one of his men is a rat. Benny's so dumb that he didn't know he had a fed in his crew. But I don't know if a girl is worth it. Benny could go down for a long, long time.

Then again, the fed seems more loyal to a Vegas crime family than the actual FBI. I half wonder if he's running them info on Benny and his goons as well.

"She's the daughter of Aaron Marks," he adds, grabbing my attention, even though I don't let him see it. "Does that sweeten the pot?"

Aaron fucking Marks. That slimy son of a bitch. He has a daughter? How the fucking hell did we miss that?

More importantly, how the hell does Benny know we have... well, *had* beef with Aaron? It was kept in-house.

He smirks, seeming to enjoy my jaw ticking and my back

stiffening. He hands me a file, and I skim it quickly, not saying anything to Benny.

Birth certificate, STI tests… There are pictures, but I bypass them when I study the part about Marks, the rat bastard son of a bitch accountant. This is actually his daughter. How the fuck did I not know he had a family?

"She doesn't know," Benny says casually. "Now she's all yours to toy with. Do we have a deal?"

It's not like I'm going to ask Benny how he knows about our grudge against the dead man. But I will be asking Pop about this shit. That's why he agreed to this. Why didn't he tell me?

Getting even with Aaron from beyond the grave will be nice, since the dick killed himself before I could kill him personally. It's also too tempting to pass up.

Without letting my eyes fall on Benny's rat and giving it away, I pull a manila envelope out of the back of my jeans and hand it to Benny. Then I sit back and watch as he reads the indisputable proof, along with pictures for a visual.

"Here she is, boss," his minion says while stepping into sight, but the girl is hidden behind Benny. All I catch a glimpse of is a delicate arm attached to soft-looking fingers.

I hope Pop breaks her. Her father sure as hell tried to fuck us nice

20

and hard.

He turns to let me see her, and my blood pumps faster the second my eyes find the innocent looking thing in front of me. Christ, she looks too damn sweet.

Jeans that are just a little too big hide her curves. Her shirt hugs her, showing me her flat stomach and fucking perfect chest. And those eyes—a shade of green that I've never seen.

She bites her lower lip as she studies me, taking me in like she's curious. Granted, I don't look like the riffraff she had bring her over here. She looks young—too young to be doing this. I might should have studied that birth certificate a little better.

"How old are you?" I ask, leaning forward to rest my elbows on my bike.

She looks around as though she's scared to speak, and that puts me on alert. I shift my gaze to Benny as my eyes narrow in suspicion.

"You sure this is of her own free will? If you're trying to pin us with a kidnapping—"

"It's of her own free will," Benny interrupts dismissively, still reading the paper in front of him as though he's soaking in all the information.

I look back to the girl who hasn't said a word, and I stare expectantly, waiting for my answer.

"Tw—twenty," she stutters, looking too nervous for this to be legit.

I glare at Benny, wondering now if this is his game.

"You realize Death Dealers are for life, right, sweetheart?" I ask, turning back to meet her scared green eyes.

We're not really lifers usually—unless you're as high up as the inner circle. As long as you keep your mouth shut, you can leave whenever if you're not in that circle. This isn't a damn street gang. But she doesn't know that.

She nods, swallowing hard, and I take a harsh breath. You can't fake that kind of fear. Living the life I have, I've seen plenty of fear in other's eyes. This is real. And I'd almost feel sorry for her if she wasn't Aaron Marks's daughter. But she is.

"Your father has the details, and she's fully aware of what she's signed on to do. She has her own reasons for this."

Benny looks up from the paperwork, and shoves it all into the back of his jeans. But when his hand comes out, there's a gun attached. His cheeks puff angrily, and a guttural growl emerges from his throat.

Fuck.

My gun is drawn before I even realize I went for it, and the sound of clicking metal rides through my ears as a wave of us do the same.

Just like hundreds of times in the past, we're facing the Hell Breathers, both sides refusing to lower their weapons as we wait on a reason to shoot.

But Benny doesn't hold his gun on me like I expected. It's pointed toward the head of his FBI informant, and I hear Sledge exhale in relief.

The guy's eyes go wide as he stares at Benny in shock, feigning innocence. Everyone around him steps wide, distancing themselves from the crazy shit.

"What are you doing?" the rat gasps, gingerly holstering his gun as a show of submission.

Stupid move. He might as well take out some of the bastards and go down in a blaze of glory. No one has pride anymore. Or balls for that matter.

My eyes rake over the newest member of our crew, and I fight the urge to shake my head in disbelief. My dad will ruin her if she's really just some girl down on her luck who had to make a deal with the devil. I half wonder if she really doesn't know about what her father did.

The question is... What's the deal she made with Benny?

"What do you mean, *Jeff*?" Benny hisses, reminding me there's about to be blood spilled. "Is this scaring you, *Jeff*? Or maybe you'd prefer to be called Adam Mason."

I don't have to look at the scene to know the fed's eyes have widened in terror. His heart is probably ready to explode. More than likely, he's on the verge of pissing his pants.

"B-Benny, don't—" Two shots silence him, but Benny doesn't stop until he's emptied the magazine.

My eyes have stayed on the girl, gauging her every reaction as she watches the fed go down. There's no way to fake that reaction, which I actually find amusing. She's terrified and... sick.

"Ah, hell," Sledge groans as the girl vomits, bending over as she loses it.

Her whole body is pale and shaking as she responds to what she probably considers a traumatic experience. It still doesn't prove that she's not being put here to spy on us, but maybe we can use her to learn more about Benny. She's weak, and the weak are easy to break.

Maybe instead of ruining her, we can use her. Obviously she's close to Benny if she came to him, which would definitely fall under the category of *spy*. We can turn her, and Benny's little plan will backfire.

"Where'd you find her?" I ask, looking back toward Benny as he curses the fed's body that lies still in a pool of his own blood.

He spits on the fed's corpse, and turns back to me as some of his guys take a few shots at the dead man as well.

"She grew up with my boy. She needed money, I needed this, and your father wants peace. It's a winning situation all around."

So he definitely knew Marks. This just raises more suspicion.

How much money does it take to have a girl hand over her body for life? It's not like the money is going to do her much good, unless she's expecting to be set free by Benny. Until we turn her on Benny, she'll never get to go anywhere or do anything—besides warm my father's bed.

That thought doesn't settle well with me now. And I really don't like the fact that I don't like it. It's hard to ignore the sour taste in my mouth.

This is our world, and I signed on for it a long time ago. Then again... Pop doesn't need to take chances. If she's supposed to be a *token of peace*, it doesn't have to be Pop's bed. Pop prefers the wild ones, anyhow.

Then again, so do I.

But if there's even a chance she might be up to something, Pop doesn't need to risk it. I'm not ready to lead the club yet, and I'm sure there are several from his second crew that would raise hell if the position fell to me prematurely. The last thing we need is a war within the outfit.

And if she *is* up to something shady, I can always fuck it out of her. Since she knows what she signed on for.

My smile grows as she staggers backwards, shielding her eyes from what's left of the gory remains.

Stepping away from all the fun and moving out of earshot, I pull out my phone, dialing my father while keeping my eyes alert.

"What's she like?" Pop asks by way of greeting, and my eyes rake back over the body of the sweet girl.

"Definitely not your usual type. But I don't want her with you. She could be their spy."

"I was already prepared for that. I have a list of fun things planned out for breaking her. Most of which will happen in the bedroom."

It shouldn't bother me—the girl is asking for it—but for some reason, the thought of Pop having her is making my stomach churn.

"She's not your style, Pop. And for all we know, she could slit your throat in your sleep. I'll keep her, see if I can find out what Benny's up to. Besides, Benny doesn't want me dead. It's you he's after right now. Let's play this smart."

His laughter creeps through the phone, and I can sense his smile.

"In other words, you want between the girl's legs. Must be a looker. You're lucky your old man has a soft spot for you, or I'd kick your ass for wanting what's mine."

I don't say anything, because I sure as hell don't want to push my luck. After a few minutes of silence, he releases a breath. "Fine. Take her. You haven't ever asked for anything, so this once I'll give you something. But don't tell her a damn thing, and see if you can figure out what Benny is after."

A lazy grin crawls into place as I turn back to face the brunette beauty who is still shaking, probably in shock. This is going to be fun.

"No worries."

"And, Drex, if she fucks up, she's dead. Understood?"

He doesn't even need to ask that.

"I'll put a bullet in her myself."

Chapter 7

EVE

He hasn't taken his eyes off me since we got here—his *clubhouse*. In fact, he's barely taken his eyes off me since he met me.

The warehouse, if that's what you can call it, is huge. As soon as you walk in, there's nothing but wide open floor space full of couches, TVs, weird art work, and even a massive kitchen off to the side. The wall against the back has doors, but two are open, leading into a red lounge type room with carpet instead of concrete.

The building is tall, big enough to be considered three stories, but there only seems to be two floors, and there's a metal, industrial-style balcony that wraps around the top, guiding the way to several doors along the path.

Large concrete columns are strategically placed along the lower level, and several large rugs are resting in various areas over the concrete floor. None of them match, but then again, neither does any of the furniture. Even the dining room table has random chairs shoved under it—and that's one hell of a massive table.

There are several sets of stairs, but Drex leads me up a set that isn't too far from the entryway, keeping me from prying farther. I follow silently, acting like the good little *gift* I am.

As I go, I ignore the curious eyes of the numerous men around. My eyes flick to a wall at the other end, all the way across from us, and I see several large garage doors that are open.

Motorcycles and cars are parked all in it, and I half wonder why Drex parked his outside instead of in there. But my thoughts are cut off as we reach a room.

It's a large room, and once we're inside, the sound of the door shutting is almost deafening, because we're alone. My life is changing, and it's changing quickly.

Is he going to leave me here for his father?

I shudder discreetly, hoping I don't get sick. Waves of nausea crash against me, battering me from the inside, but I do my best to remain an external picture of composure.

Even though this room is big, there's not a lot in it. One large dresser, one large closet, a massive bed, several odd angles—that could be perfect for hiding—and what appears to be a bathroom.

The walls are cold and hard, just like Drex.

Drex is the Vice President and son of Herrin—President of the Death Dealers—and I'm actually surprised. I'm surprised about Drex being VP, not Herrin being President.

Drex is maybe in his late twenties, but he doesn't look anything like what I expected a VP to look like. He doesn't look polished, but he doesn't look like he just rolled out of bed either.

This isn't the type of MC that just hangs out and loves to ride together on occasion. This isn't the happy-go-lucky type of group that look like killers but are secretly Teddy Bears. No. This is an organization, a business, and an elite team of criminals who have banded together, just like the Hell Breathers. And now I know for a fact that they're killers.

Coldhearted killers.

These are the lethal criminals; motorcycles just happen to be involved.

Drex isn't bearded like some of them. He has just enough stubble to pull off that slacker sexy. His soft, dark hair is short on the sides, almost buzzed, but the top is long enough to run your fingers through and have something to tug. Though the only reason I want to tug it is to use it as a handle to hold him still while I knee his balls and run away.

Unfortunately, I'd rather live—at least one more day.

He's tall, like at least 6'3. Even though it's hot outside, he's wearing a leather jacket that has "Death Dealers" proudly displayed on the back. There are several skull symbol things embroidered on the jacket that apparently represent their club, along with a grim reaper in the center of them.

On his right hand, his fingers are tattooed near the base, with the exception of his thumb. DREX is spelled out, as though he wants someone to see his name before his fist connects.

"Eve Marks?" he asks, intrigued, and it shakes me from my inner appraisal.

I just nod as he chuckles, circling me as he reads from the file Benny apparently gave him. I'm not sure what exactly he finds amusing. How much of my personal information is in there?

Though he's beautifully disguised, he's a monster just like the rest of them. I've never seen anyone die right in front of my eyes, especially not so brutally, but they all seemed to either enjoy it, or they acted bored. This creep watched me the whole time, probably enjoying how sick it all made me.

I need therapy now.

Alcohol would be a good substitute, since I doubt this group has a therapist on hand.

I'm not sure if I'm still in shock, or maybe staying in denial, or if it's just survival mode, but I've pushed the entire scene from my head, refusing to fully let the reality sink in.

He drops the file on the table in the bedroom, and the loud clap it produces forces me to startle just a bit. I recover quickly as he crosses his arms over his chest while he studies me.

"What does Benny want to learn about us?" he asks, his voice deceptively calm.

Huh?

"What?" I ask in a hoarse rasp, inwardly cringing at how terrified I sound.

I hope he doesn't confuse terror for guilt. I'm not sure what he's probing for right now, but I certainly don't want him thinking I'm working for Benny.

"Come on, Eve," he says with a lazy drawl, letting my name roll off his tongue. "It's not every day a girl from the suburbs crashes into a clubhouse and offers herself up to be used and traded. In fact, it's probably the first time I've personally heard of it. So what does Benny have on you, and what does he want? Either he's blackmailing you over some dark, dirty secret. Or you're here because you're one of those girls who is going through a curious, rebellious phase. Believe me, darlin', this isn't the place for a phase."

Regardless of my answer, it's too late now. Benny would kill me if the Death Dealers didn't kill me first. I've signed myself over to be at their disposal—consequences be damned.

I suppose I'll be damned, too.

And I hate being called *darling*.

Deciding not to mention that, mostly because I don't want to piss him off, I answer honestly. "I needed mone—"

"Don't," he interrupts, waving his hand for emphasis. "Money isn't why you're doing this. If you want money this way, you prostitute yourself out to classy businessmen. With a face like yours, you'd be with the high class hookers, making more than enough money. Here, you won't be getting to use that money too often. For as long as you can think, this is your new home."

A tear begs to fall, but I deny it the right. "Prostituting myself out wouldn't have gotten the money as soon as I needed it. My mom was about to lose the house, and my brothers start school this year. She was on the verge of losing everything."

For a fleeting moment, his expression softens, but almost as quickly, the hard, emotionless glower is back.

"So you're saying you did this for your family. That's your story?" He pauses, and I nod, deciding to rest my tremulous voice. "Well, as sweet as that sounds, I reserve the right to be suspicious. Guys like us don't make trades for peace."

He walks around me, and my breath catches in my throat, becoming painfully lodged when he touches me just at my collarbone. Though his touch is gentle and not inappropriate, it's a reminder that soon his father will be touching me in places that aren't so innocent.

His finger trails over my chest, slowly heading south, going between my breasts, and stopping right at the top of my jeans, hovering over the button.

"You should strip. These clothes aren't going to cut it. And I also need to search you. Everywhere."

Everywhere. That word echoes through my mind, crashing back at me as though it's a warning.

He removes his hand and steps away, watching and waiting, and I swallow hard. The painful knot in my throat only grows as I reach for the hem of my shirt. Taking a deep breath, I pull it off quickly.

His eyes are on me, watching with open interest as I move to my jeans. As much as I'd like to draw this out and delay the inevitable, I also don't want to keep dreading the first time. The sooner I'm naked, the sooner the suspense ends. I've prepared myself for what I hope is the worst.

"You know what's going to happen to you, right?" he asks, crossing his arms over his chest as I push the jeans down my legs. He takes a deep breath as I step out of them. In nothing but my pink, cotton underwear, I try to find the courage to meet his gaze, keeping my expression as impassive as possible under the grim circumstances.

"I know."

His lips twitch with amusement, and I reach for the clasp of my bra, trembling harder as it comes undone.

"And this is consensual?" he asks, acting as though he gives a damn.

"Would it matter if it wasn't?" I retort, my eyes growing wide with fearful regret.

Shit. Why did I say that?

His eyes darken as he studies me, and I drop the bra to the ground, baring my breasts, and hoping that's enough to distract him. His father is about to do as he wants with my body. It's stupid as hell to piss off his son right now.

His eyes dart down to my breasts, and his dark smile barely returns.

"If this isn't consensual—completely consensual—you're going back to Benny. I don't have to force girls into my bed. And the second you give your consent, you're mine any time, any place, and any way I want. This is your one and only chance to walk away. Understood?"

His? I'm his? I thought I was going to his father.

Deciding against voicing that—since a guy closer to my age is preferable to some perverted old bastard—I nod.

"I understand," I murmur, ignoring the surging adrenaline in my body. If I'm going to be his, then... This is about to happen. Shit.

Hooking my thumbs in the sides of my panties, I shimmy them down my legs, ignoring my desire to cover myself as I straighten back up. He appraises me, putting me on a level beneath him as he stays clothed and keeps that scrutinizing gleam in his blue eyes.

"Turn around and put your hands on the top of the mattress," he says, his voice commanding but restrained and husky, as though he's holding himself back.

Nausea sweeps over me again, but I fight it back as I turn and do what he wants me to. My hands shake with crippling fear as I push them against the mattress, and his breath comes suddenly, surprising me at my ear as his shirt tickles against my bare back.

"I've got to search you." His velvety, smooth, deep voice shouldn't be seductive. He's a criminal, a coldhearted killer, and I'm about to let him touch me without true protest.

"Open your mouth and spread your legs," he orders.

Even though my knees try to buckle, I immediately obey, and he reaches around me, putting his middle finger into my mouth. He circles his digit around, inspecting each crevice as though he might find something. I try not to gag, because even though that finger tastes good, I have no idea where it has been.

After a lot of probing in my mouth, he withdraws his hand, and it disappears from sight. He warned me he would touch me, but he never said where. When his wet finger—lubed with my own saliva—slips into a place that's never been touched, I try to jerk away out of instinct.

"Don't. Move," he growls in my ear, bringing his other large hand to wrap around my waist, spreading his fingers over my stomach and hip, firmly holding me against him as he probes me.

There's no real pain, but the feeling is so alien and... uncomfortable, especially since I've known him for just minutes. He pushes in a little deeper, and I suck in a breath, feeling his finger touch places I didn't consider would get touched. I suppose I only thought I was prepared for the worst.

I really hope his finger is all he puts up there.

"You've never been touched back here, have you?" he asks, his lips close enough to graze my ear. The denim of his jeans scratches against my skin as he pushes even closer, letting me feel the hard outline of proof this is turning him on.

I swallow down my panic while trying to answer, but my voice breaks and some squeaky sound comes out instead. So I shake my head *no* to answer.

His throaty chuckle is mocking me, but I can't really focus on it when he pulls his finger out and swaps hands. The hand that was just violating me moves to be on my waist, restraining me, while his other comes between my legs to cup me.

My rush of breath falls out as his finger slips inside me, and that's when I feel my body has betrayed me. Shit.

"Turned on?" he muses, sliding his finger through the wet slit, a teasing, slow motion that makes my stomach muscles clench in response.

Silence is the best reaction to that question. I'm not turned on, but my body doesn't understand what's going on. It doesn't know the—

"I can't get deep enough to give you a thorough search this way. You're on birth control, right? I'm not using a condom with you."

A cold sweat breaks out as those words resonate. My body trembles for reasons that confuse me as conflicting emotions rattle around. I shouldn't feel excited, but I do. I should be appalled and in tears, not quivering in anticipation of the promised debauchery.

The contradictory myriad of sensations strike me with guilt and disgust until an internal war threatens to emerge.

"I am," I whisper, unable to find a stronger tone.

He laughs again, a low rumble that seems to vibrate through my body as the sound of a belt being undone turns up the tension. I hold myself still, refusing to look behind me. I'm afraid to breathe.

"Don't worry. You'll love every second of it," he says against my ear, and my knees tremble as his warm skin brushes against me from behind, letting me know his shirt is already gone. "By the time I'm done with you, you'll beg for more."

It wouldn't be smart to tell him that's the most insane thing I've ever heard, so I keep my mouth shut and let him fuel his own ego. A hard knot forms in my throat when the blunt tip of his cock prods my entrance, and he coats the head in the traitorous wetness that has pooled between my legs. He toys with my entrance, teasing me, torturing me, and I inwardly curse the way my stomach tightens again in anticipation instead of roiling in disgust.

Just the tip slides in, and I freaking moan like a sick pervert. Clamping my mouth shut, I try to ignore the sensations that swarm me and the disappointment I feel when he withdraws.

"Oh fuck," I blurt out when he rams into me suddenly and silences my thoughts.

"So fucking wet," he growls low in my ear, staying inside me. "I think you like danger, sweet girl. I think it turns you the fuck on. This is going to be more fun than I thought."

I don't have more time than that to adjust to the ungodly size of the intruder inside me before he pulls back and thrusts forward again, forcing my body to surge forth and slam into the side of the bed.

There's no hesitation before his body continues the brutal punishment. "Too fucking tight," he hisses, grabbing a handful of flesh on my ass as he pounds in once again, forcing an ungraceful grunt from my lips.

It's only just not painful, and I hate the fact that my body is reacting in a way I wasn't prepared for. I want to cry when I start feeling pleasure, because this isn't supposed to feel good.

I whimper when he bites down on my shoulder, pushing his body flush with mine as his hips continue to buck without mercy. Roughly, he tugs my hair back, forcing my head at an odd angle as he makes his claim on my body.

His other hand travels around to my front, sliding across that bundle of nerves, and he starts a circular pattern that forces me up onto my toes, as an involuntary moan comes out once more. He bites down harder on my shoulder, offering pain and pleasure at the same time, as his body writhes with mine.

I push back against him when my body seizes control and excludes my mind from the process. He growls as he meets me push for push, our bodies colliding forcefully. I've never been fucked like this, and I hate him for making me love it.

"Scream. I want to hear you scream," he growls against my ear, and with just the right amount of pressure where I need it, my body spirals in a mutinous orgasm that almost forces me to black out.

I'm a freak. I never knew I was a freak.

As cries of pleasure escape me in the scream he demanded, I learn more about what a twisted freak I really am.

My body continues to convulse around him, clenching tightly around his cock, and he breathes harshly, expelling curses as though they're high praise. He continues to slam into me so forcefully that it lifts me up, extending my own orgasm until it's almost painfully sensitive. The slapping sound from his skin to mine is loud, and the air is a heady rush that could get the sober high.

Suddenly, his motions go from hard thrusts to concentrated jerks, and his bruising grip on my ass lessens just as he releases some sexy, guttural groan.

He pulls out of me as quickly as he entered, and I feel a sense of hollowness in place of where he was. Ignoring that pang of disappointment at the loss of contact so abruptly becomes my primary focus.

I hear the rustle of his jeans as I sink to the floor, my back still turned, as the shame washes over me. The wetness between my thighs is a mixture of him and me, keeping reality fresh in my mind. I'm still trying to process all this.

"Get your clothes on. One of the girls will get you more stuff to wear. You can't ride with us in your preppy girl attire. You'll draw too much attention."

I just nod weakly while hugging myself.

41

"And do that pouting, crying shit, and I'll go ahead and give you back to Benny. I don't need that drama. Buzz kill."

The callous, cold nature of his tone isn't surprising, but it still cuts me. I sniffle and nod quickly while standing to my feet. I start picking up my clothes, wondering if any of my dignity is left within the fabric.

"Look at me and tell me you understand."

I swallow hard, and then I bring my eyes to slowly climb up his body. His jeans are back on, but he's barefoot, and the top button on his pants is open. His shirt is in his hand, giving my eyes a new sight.

The hard lines of his abdomen and chest are… distracting. His arms are sleeved with tattoos, and several more are on his chest and sides. A flicker of silver catches my eyes, and I realize he has a barbell through each nipple.

Honestly, I've never seen a pierced nipple before this moment. Not that it's more than a second-long distraction.

Finally, my eyes meet his piercing blue ones, and I ignore the cocky grin on his face.

"You're not to touch anyone else here. If you're going to be mine, then you're only mine."

It's actually a relief to know he won't be passing me around.

"And you?" I ask, cursing myself for being so brazen.

His brow cocks in amusement as one corner of his mouth quirks up in a taunting grin.

"What about me?" he asks, but I look down instead of answering.

"Answer me," he prompts. "And look at me while you speak."

Slowly, I bring my eyes back up.

"Are you only going to be touching me?"

He laughs as he comes closer, a mocking sound once again.

This man just fucked me so thoroughly that I can barely stand, and he never even bothered to kiss me. I'm not sure why that's the center of my focus right now. There are other things much larger to worry about.

He grabs my chin roughly, but not painfully, and tilts my head up as he runs his free hand down my naked side, slowly moving to my ass when he gets close enough.

"I'm Drex Caine, baby. I'll touch whoever I want, whenever I want."

Which means I'll go to the doctor regularly.

I don't speak. Instead, I hold his gaze and let him intimidate me the way he wants to. I won't fight him in any way, because he'll consider it a challenge and try to break me.

I'll let him win all the battles so that I can endure the war.

"Stay up here. I have to go meet with Pop. Don't come down."

Considering there is an entire warehouse below that is full of bikers that scare the hell out of me, I'm glad he's leaving me up here. But what would be the consequences if I didn't follow orders?

"Will I be staying up here?" I ask weakly. "I mean… full time. Is this my room?"

His dark smile shouldn't be so sexy. In fact, it makes me hate him more, because I feel all the more twisted for liking that smile.

"This is my room, but yeah. You'll stay up here for now. Until I decide what to do with you. You can sleep over there." He points to a leather couch against the far wall of the vast room.

Two girls with their legs spread wide, heads thrown back mid-orgasm, and bodies bare for all to see, are on a poster that adorns the wall just above that couch.

I really hope he has disinfectant spray or something.

"Okay."

"Blankets are in the closet. Sheets, too. And you can take one of the pillows from my bed. Just one."

I nod while tucking my head low. I brought my own pillow in my bag, along with my own blankets, just in case I got lucky enough to have my own bed. A couch is better than sharing a bed. And I guess it's better Drex has me instead of his father. My skin isn't crawling like I thought it would be. Which is another set of issues I'll have to deal with. Later.

If I survive this, I'm going to need *a lot* of therapy.

"Thank you," I say, not bothering to tell him I have all my own things.

"Your bags are downstairs. I'll have Sledge bring them up. Have your clothes on before he comes up here."

I start pulling on my panties immediately, even though I need to clean up. I'm still riddled with exhaustion after our brief encounter and in need of a post-sex shower.

He turns and walks away, and I suck in a sharp breath. His back has even more tattoos than his front. Massive, intricate patterns of ink barely leave much flesh to be seen.

The grim reaper is in a pit of fire, the flames rolling across his back like an ominous warning. That's what was wrapping around his sides—flames.

I'm still staring as he walks away, pulling on his shirt as he goes. He leaves me behind as the door shuts, and my eyes immediately soak in my surroundings a little better once he's not distracting me.

This room could serve as an apartment.

I scoop up my clothes and rush into the bathroom. After Sledge comes and goes, I'll take a shower. In fact, I'll just hide in the bathroom until he leaves.

The less his people get to see me, the safer I'll feel.

Chapter 8

DREX

The twisted grin on my face might stay there for a while. I'm going to enjoy this more than I thought. Didn't realize how much I liked the sweet ones until right now, and she's sure as hell sweet. I guess time will tell how much like her father she is.

That sobering thought sours my good mood. So much for my fucking smile sticking around.

"Drex." Sledge's gruff voice reminds me I came this way for a reason.

"Sledge, grab the girl's bags and put them in my room. And don't hang around to talk to her."

I don't want anyone speaking to her when I'm not around. That way I can monitor every tidbit of information she has, and I can figure out if or when she tries to use it against us. I've already confiscated her phone, and she didn't bring any other electronic devices—we searched her shit before we even loaded her up on the back of my bike.

Sledge frowns as he glances up toward my apartment. This garage

47

holds several different rooms, but since Pop left, I took the biggest. The downstairs is the biggest area—full of cars and bikes. We only stay here when we have a heavy workload. It keeps our merchandise safe. No one fucks with us, especially when we're all together.

"Herrin's going to be pissed if you just did what I think you did. Damn, boy. Are you stupid?"

I smirk as I glance down at my watch.

"Pop agreed that she might be a risk. I'm keeping her until we figure out what's going on."

He rolls his eyes as he grabs her bags. "When Herrin sees her, he's going to kick your ass. Girl's not ugly. He'll feel duped."

I shrug carelessly. "I told him exactly what she looks like. It's too much to risk. Benny's not after me. If that's his plan—to get close to Pop—then this will be perfect. I'll play while they get no info and no shot at our President."

"So you're staking claim?" he asks, amused as he glances back up at the door.

I don't like the way he words that question, so I refuse to answer him.

"Call Cecil. Tell him I want an appointment for two tomorrow."

Sledge chuckles long and hard, and he throws the last bag over his shoulder.

"Damn. Must have been good. I'll call him."

It's not about how good it was. It's a matter of property.

***

"You'll let me know if she gives you anything," Pop says, taking another bite of his steak as I drink my beer.

"Yes, Sir."

He chews slowly as he studies me. "But you think she might be telling the truth?"

I shrug with one shoulder as my eyes rake over the new shipment list we have to get out undetected.

"Too soon to tell, but the girl was scared to damn death in the bedroom. If she's a spy, she's a damn good actress. It's doubtful she knows anything about Benny and his shitheads. I know Benny has something planned, but I don't know what. He may be planning on using the girl in the future."

"I never knew Marks had a kid," Pop says around a mouthful. "Or a wife. Or a fucking family. No one can hide shit from me, but he somehow did. Remember she's his daughter, so she could be just as skilled at concealing the truth as he was."

49

My jaw tics at just the mention of her father's name.

"I wonder if he lied to his family and kept secrets from them just as well as he kept them from us?" I ask, more to myself than to him.

"It's a strong possibility. But she's linked to Benny somehow."

I nod, remembering where I was going with my earlier statement.

"She's saying her mom was hurting for cash and about to lose her house. Benny knows her family, so—"

"So you think he might be planning to take advantage and use them as leverage against her later on. Smart. Sounds a little like a conspiracy theory, but still worth looking into. You got someone on her family to keep an eye out? I want to know what this bastard does before he does it. This girl may afford us the element of surprise as long as we keep playing dumb. I don't know how else Benny would have known about Marks and what he did. It can't be just a coincidence he knows her family."

Benny and Aaron a team? "I don't believe in coincidences. Benny never got paid if they were working together, since we got all the money back. This could be part of his plan—see if she can get the access her father had. But he'd have to know he was showing his hand, because he realizes we're not idiots."

He nods, his mind already working over something. "He surely wouldn't think we'd be stupid enough to give her any access, given her father's name. It's a puzzle to solve."

I stand and walk over to the very noticeable coolers. Pop shouldn't have this shit in his apartment. One raid and he's in the pin. Instead of voicing the fact this shit is pissing me off, I continue talking about the matter at hand.

"Juice and Evan are going to set up shop across the street from her mom. The house there was empty. It's now Death Dealer property. If Benny makes a move, we'll know it. If he goes for her family, then we'll have all the ammo we need to start a war. I still think we should take him out now and be done with it."

Pop laughs long and hard, acting as though I'm his entertainment for the evening. "Boy, you'd kill every rival club if you could. That's why I let you keep the girl. You've earned it, and hell, you could use the distraction. We can't go starting wars. Everyone you kill has someone who wants revenge. We kill when there isn't another option."

I cock an eyebrow.

"I thought I was keeping the girl because we agreed it was safer."

I don't like his condescending smirk. "No, that's just what you're telling yourself. You want her. That's fine by me. I've got plenty to keep me busy. Besides, Esmeralda is getting jealous these days. She's under the delusion she can make me settle down. A girl as innocent as you've described would have her eyes clawed out within minutes around here. Best she stay and keep your bed full."

I frown as I sit back down. "She's on my couch until I find her a room. I sleep alone."

"My apologies," he says with that same thick condescension. "She can keep your couch warm. Just so you know, it's easier to fuck them in the bed. Couches are for teenagers."

Rolling my eyes, I stand and head to the window. Two unmarked cars are parked just below. Feds are watching us now, but this isn't news.

Turning around, I nudge a cooler with my foot while asking, "What're you going to do with the drugs if they come in?"

Pop waves me off like it's no big deal.

"It's just a cooler full. I'll flush the shit if it comes to that. No worries. If they had a search warrant, they'd have already charged in like the cavalier asses they are." The knife scratches the surface of the plate as he readies a new bite of steak. "I want you to keep me posted on the girl. If she's innocent, try not to torture her too much, just in case we have to use her later on. We'll want her compliant and not overly resentful."

I smirk as I head toward the door. "No worries, Pop."

Torture isn't what I have in mind.

Chapter 9

EVE

Two girls with long, silky hair walk in, carrying bags of what appears to be clothing. One girl has auburn hair that can't be natural. The other is a platinum blonde with perfectly manicured red nails.

They don't look the way I expected. I guess I expected fake bimbos with boobs spilling out of their tops and gum hanging out of their mouths. They look chic and understated sexy. I'd even say they look classy.

The wall dips and has a hidden cove. This is the safest place in the room to stay hidden. They haven't seen me, but I can see them through the reflection of the mirror on the adjacent wall.

"So Drex, like, bought the girl or something?" the redhead asks. "Didn't realize the sex slave ring was back in style."

"He didn't buy the girl," a gruff voice says, matching the man who brought my stuff up earlier while I hid in the bathroom.

He announced himself as Sledge when he came in, but I stayed hidden and silent until he left.

"So…" The blonde's words trail off as she awaits an answer.

"It's a long story. She should be up here, so let's not discuss it. She's probably hiding in the bathroom again." He sounds… worried? Perhaps sympathetic? I'm not sure. He doesn't sound cold though.

Both girls are thin with tight jeans on. They look like normal, gorgeous women, but they have matching tattoos on their inner wrists—the initials *DD*. The font is bold and the letters are large, making it easy to see even through the mirror. As long as I don't move, they won't notice me in the mirror—unless they look at it, of course.

I've made myself as small as possible, curling into a ball almost.

"We don't need to be dealing with human trafficking shit. Other than the fact it's archaic and sick, the feds are watching us enough as it is. They've been at the salon all week. They keep coming in for haircuts they don't need, and asking questions they think we're stupid enough to answer truthfully. Someone is feeding them information, because they know too many of the right questions to ask. I'm not so sure some chick getting sold to the club is the greatest idea, considering the convenient circumstances," the girl continues, baiting him.

Sledge cracks his neck to the side and glances toward the bathroom door that is closed.

"It's not a damn human trafficking thing. It is… a unique

situation, but I don't want to explain it here. We'll discuss this downstairs. Does Drex know about the feds snooping around?"

"Called him the first day they came in," the redhead says.

They proceed with pulling all the clothes out of the bags, and they tuck them into the drawers, moving very slowly, proving they're in no rush.

"If they're scoping out the salon, they're probably watching this place, too. But they're apparently being more discreet than they are over at Herrin's spot. I should call Drex," he tells them.

Sledge turns to leave, and I hold back the waves of nausea. Why does the FBI want them? Because of the guy I had to watch be killed?

Swallowing hard, I push down the bile-encrusted memory that tries to surface. In one traumatic day, I sold my body to monsters, I was bent over a bed by a man I didn't know, my body responded to him in the most traitorous of ways, and I had to watch a man's head get blown off.

As much as I'd love to stay in this corner for the rest of my time here—however long that might be—the words Drex said keep running through my mind.

I can't pout. I can't act like this is as horrible as it is. I'm expected to play a part, or he'll send me to Benny. The hairs on my body rise at the mere thought of something that vile. There's no telling what he would do to me if I got sent back.

This all stinks to hell and back. I'm starting to feel like a pawn, especially since they all seem to be just as leery of this peculiar situation as I am. I thought it was a common occurrence amongst them. Apparently this is just as frigging crazy and unusual as I found it to be.

But what could Benny possibly have to gain by doing this? And why would Drex and his crew play along if it's so out of the ordinary?

Their conversation grows louder when the redhead says, "Drex hasn't ever had to pay for ass before. Why would he start now?"

They're still hanging up my clothes or neatly folding them into drawers.

"He's not paying for shit. The girl was a gift. Christ, why won't you just come downstairs and talk about it? There's no reason we have to discuss it up here."

Sledge sounds irritated now, and his eyes keep flicking to the bathroom where he thinks I am. The small mirror still gives me a decent view of all three of them, though I hope they don't glance in its direction. They might tell Drex I was hiding in the corner, and I'm pretty sure he wouldn't like that.

"Because we're waiting to see her. I'm assuming Drex will want her working at the salon or at the massage parlor. I'd like to at least know what the girl looks like. The longer we stand out here and talk, the sooner she warms up and comes to answer some questions for herself," the blonde says, eyeing Sledge very defiantly with a broad smile on her face.

The guy is a beast. No way in hell would I talk to him like that. Is she crazy?

"Drex doesn't want anyone talking to her. So I doubt she'll be working with you. And I'm sure he doesn't want everyone up here getting to know her. If you'll come downstairs, I'll explain that better."

He doesn't want anyone talking to me? Great. I've apparently sold myself and turned into a sex-slave prisoner. I'm starting to realize there's no amount of therapy in the world that will be able to save me after this is over.

If it's ever over.

"What the hell's going on up here?"

Drex's voice forces a blanket of dread and nerves to cloak me and almost strangle me. Shit. He's here. He'll see me being the miserable girl in the corner.

I need to put on my game face and act like I'm able to handle this. But that's exactly what it'll be—an act.

Chapter 10

DREX

I gave one simple order—don't speak to the damn girl. I heard them talking from all the way downstairs. Un-fucking-believable. Just because she's hiding in the bathroom, that doesn't mean she's not listening in.

I glare at Sledge, and he mumbles something about stubborn women. He needs to grow a set. He's too big to be such a fucking pushover.

"I said, what the hell is going on up here?" I snap, glaring at Colleen, Sarah, and Sledge like they're idiots. Because they are.

The girls both look down immediately, and Sledge groans. "The girls were curious about your new toy. They thought she might be working at the salon or the spa."

The salon and spa are two of the legitimate businesses we use to clean the money we make on our car rebuilds and transports. Considering we can't exactly let the feds walk in and see the cars and bikes we gut and rebuild to hide drugs or guns for transports, we need clean businesses that we can cook the books on.

Too much shit goes on in both places for the possible spy to head in to work. Besides, she'd have access to Benny too easily if I let her out of my sight.

"She's not working. Get your asses out of my space, and get downstairs. I'll discuss this with you later."

Colleen practically sprint out, Sarah skips away, and Sledge flips off their backs as he follows.

I glance over some of the clothes they've put in the closet. It's a hell of a lot better than the preppy shit she has. The second the feds get a glimpse of her with her sweet-and-innocent grandma clothes, they'll ask questions. They're already going to be curious about a new girl.

"Eve," I call, glancing at some of the sexy panties and bras the girls bought.

Much better than the old lady underwear she had on earlier. Even if she still looked plenty sexy.

I'm going to have more fun with her in lace.

"Yeah," she says, suddenly right behind me.

I turn quickly, measuring her carefully. She's wearing my shirt, and that forces me to arch a brow.

"Why were you hiding? And why are you wearing my shirt?"

She doesn't look overly stressed out, which is disconcerting. After the hellacious day, she'd be freaking out if she was as sweet and innocent as I originally thought.

"I wasn't hiding. I was trying to be respectful. I wasn't given permission to speak to anyone else, and you mentioned that you hated my clothes. Since I had nothing else at the time, I borrowed a shirt in case you came back."

What the...

Is she for real?

Emotionless. She's so stoic that it's actually a little creepy.

Her eyes glisten with unshed tears suddenly, and I tilt my head. "You look like you're about to cry," I murmur absently, still studying the soft green eyes.

It sort of pisses me off that she's about to cry, because she seemed fine two seconds ago.

"I'm fine," she lies, turning her head as she moves over to the dresser. "What would you prefer I wore?"

This whole master/servant thing isn't doing it for me. "Whatever they bought. You just can't wear your shit. Too many questions will rise. Now, tell me why you're about to cry."

I glare at her back, waiting for an answer. She was fine until I showed up, and I know for a fact I haven't done shit to her. She sure as hell enjoyed herself earlier, and I asked repeatedly if it was all consensual.

"It's just been an overwhelming day. I'm sorry. I swear I'm not going to cry," she says with her back turned, her body close to shaking. "I've never seen anyone die, I left my family, and… I swear I'm okay. Don't send me back to Benny."

Her voice stays steady throughout that little explanation. Until she reaches the last sentence. That's when it breaks.

Is she scared of Benny? Does he have something on her that I don't know about? And how the fuck does she know him?

"So you're doing this for your family," I say, dropping to the bed as she selects a pair of cut-off shorts and a white shirt.

She swallows audibly while turning to face me. "Yes. You're welcome to check my family's financial history."

Already have someone looking into that, baby.

"And what would happen if I just turned you loose and sent you back home to your family?" I ask, smirking when her head pops up in surprise.

For a fleeting second, she looks so hopeful. I'm learning a lot just from her expressions. But then her face falls.

She sighs as she reaches for the bottom hem of her shirt—well, my shirt—and pulls it over her head. No fucking underwear. Now I'm distracted as hell, and I slowly slide to the edge of the bed, moving to be just beside where she has laid out the selection of clothing.

"Stay naked while you speak," I tell her, feeling like a bit of an ass with that command, but not giving a damn.

Her body tenses, but she doesn't argue. At all.

"If you were to set me free this early, Benny would think I'd screwed up and pissed you off or begged to be set free. Possibly think I was inadequate. I honestly don't know, but I know he wouldn't just let me return home and pretend as though I don't have a debt to pay."

The fear is real. Or else she's a hell of an actress. But she seems more afraid of Benny than she does me. Appearances can be deceiving. I make Benny look amateur. But maybe she's afraid for another reason.

Benny might actually go and kill her family. Perhaps he's already threatened to. He wants something, and she's the center of it all. I just have to keep an eye on him and wait for him to make his move.

"How'd a girl like you run into a guy like Benny?" I ask, unable to keep my hands off her any longer.

Her soft skin has been on my mind all day. Softest damn thing I've ever felt. Her curves are placed in all the right places, and her beautiful tits will fuck with my head even after I've had my fill of her.

I tug her to me, pulling her down until she's straddling my lap. Her pebbled nipples are the first clue that she's not exactly immune to me—by any means. Even though she's wary, she can't seem to help herself.

My mouth moves over her nipple, and her breath leaves in a harsh rush as she grips onto my shoulders.

"I asked you a question," I remind her softly, moving my attention to her other nipple as she tries to find the ability to form words.

"I know Ben. His son. We went to school together. He took me to his dad when I needed help. Benny gave me this one and only option."

Her head falls back as her legs spread wider, and she allows herself to sink down on me fully.

So she's friends with the boy that doesn't have the stomach for our work. I can actually picture that.

Her dark hair falls forward when she leans into me, and I tilt my head, barely holding back a small laugh. She wants to kiss me. Interesting.

I smirk as I flip her to be on the bed, and her eyes widen in surprise.

"You should keep something in mind," I say as I stand up, pulling my shirt over my head.

Her eyes go to my stomach, slowly sliding down to my waist where I've started undoing my jeans. Her chest rises and falls more rapidly as her breaths increase, and I take my time. Once I've shed my jeans, I walk back over to her, letting her soak in the sight of me as I crawl over her body.

I tilt her head up as I poise the tip of my cock at her soaking wet entrance. Her sharp intake of air is erotic as hell when I press just a little more inside her. Fuck, she's so damn tight.

"You don't want to cross me," I say, teasing her lower lip with my thumb as I push my cock inside her just a little farther.

The fact she's this turned on with very little effort is fucking killing me.

Biting back a groan, I try to keep my composure, waiting on her to respond.

"I'm not going to," she whispers, arching her hips almost involuntarily as a war goes on behind her eyes.

I pull back and slam into her, forcing her back to bow off the bed, and a cry of pleasure to fall from her lips. She's pretty fucking beautiful—especially right now.

"Good," I growl, picking up a powerful rhythm that has her clamping her legs around my waist. "Because if you think Benny is scary, you'll be fucking terrified of me."

Fear flashes through her eyes, and for a brief second, I almost feel guilty. But when her walls clench and damn near strangle my cock, I see her struggling even more with the war within her. Lust, confusion, and fear all teem inside her fuck-me eyes.

Danger excites her.

I really like the fact I just threatened her and she's turned on enough to cry out again. I drop my head to watch her, enjoying the way her eyes go lazy and her expression gets sexier, more relaxed as she just rides out the pleasure.

Each stroke gets tighter as her orgasm hits her, causing her muscles to contract. Her pussy squeezing my cock in another iron-grip as she comes hard and cries out is the last of my restraint.

Holy. Shit.

My balls tighten as a searing shot of pleasure burns through my toes and up through my spine. I've never gotten off so fucking hard.

Best *gift* ever.

Dropping to her, I let my lips just barely miss hers. I've never been so tempted to kiss a girl as I am right now. The fact she's scared and turned on is really messing with my head and my cock.

I refrain from the temptation and turn my head to the side instead of acting like an idiot who's caught up in the moment.

"Ben isn't your friend any longer," I say against the pillow, feeling her stiffen beneath me. "Death Dealers don't play with Hell Breathers. Or any other clubs for that matter. You'll learn the rules as you go, but that's the number one rule."

I lean up to see her lower lip trembling. She'd better not have feelings for him. That could put a bigger kink in this whole situation. But that's something I need to explore. The more we know about her, the better.

She nods her agreement, and I pull out of her, watching as she winces from the loss of the connection and a breath of air hisses between her teeth. As I grab my pants, I toss her the clothes she just picked out. If she doesn't put something on, I'm going to keep fucking her all day. And I've got a plan to put into action.

"Get dressed and meet me downstairs in twenty minutes," I tell her, watching her green eyes go wide.

I chuckle lightly while pulling on my jeans, bypassing my boxers just to drive her a little crazier.

"You can't stay up here all the time."

She swallows hard but nods. She's almost being too compliant. That only makes me more suspicious of her.

"Twenty minutes. Not a minute before or a minute after."

That's demanding enough for her to argue the complexity of such a request. But instead, she looks at the clock and nods again.

Biting back the questions I'd like to ask, I turn and head out the door. If I ask too much too soon, I won't find out a damn thing. I wish Pop would just let me blow Benny and his club all to hell. Then I could save myself from this very elaborate game.

Chapter 11

DREX

"Financial shit checks out," Axle says as he walks in.

I glance up to the top of the stairs. It won't be long until she comes down. Right now it's just me and the top five. The other girls will be back shortly, since I sent them to go grab food while we talked.

"So her family suddenly inherited a bit of cash from the Hell Breathers?"

"Half a million," he answers, and Sledge whistles low and loud.

"Thought we were the only ones hauling in enough cash to drop that much on something as pointless as this," Sledge says while shaking his head.

Benny is apparently making more money than we thought if he can spend half a mill on a *gift* for us.

"No way this girl doesn't have strings. I say we cut her loose now and deal with Benny," Dash says, running a hand over the spiky blue tips of his short fauxhawk.

"Not happening. Pop doesn't want to start a war. We could lose some of our allies, and we might gain more enemies. He wants proof Benny is up to something, so that when we start a war, no one thinks it's a power struggle. It has to look like vengeance to keep anyone from getting antsy."

They all nod, agreeing. Too many clubs would likely come after us if they thought we targeted Benny's club and then obligated his crew to fight back. They'd be worried they were next, so that would mean Benny would be rewarded with more allies, and we'd gather more enemies.

Maybe that's his game.

Not to mention all the damn street gangs that are in the outlying bigger cities who would get worried about us trying to take over and kill for power. The drug and gun trade is more lucrative than ever, but it's also more dangerous than ever.

"So we keep the girl and find out what Benny is up to?" Mack asks, leaning forward.

I don't like the look he's giving the door to my room. He's usually at Pop's place, not here. He tends to forget to show me respect.

"*We* don't keep the girl. *I* keep the girl. No one else is to touch her."

He scowls as I check my watch. Just a few more minutes. We have to get this wrapped up before she comes down.

"Hurry up and run through the worry list. Just like with all the girls that come over or work for us, we only talk legit shit in front of her."

They all nod in agreement, and Snake leans forward. "We got ten of the cars done today. Harrison is coming by to take a look tomorrow. He'll bring the other half of the payment. Should we be worried about doing this with the Feds hanging around?"

I shake my head, propping my elbows up on my knees. "We're only using a couple of kilos for the demonstration. We can flush that quickly with no problem. If the feds try coming in, they won't find our basement garage. Besides, they don't have shit for a warrant or they would have already come in."

They nod, and I continue.

"We'll use the new underground passage to get our clients through to the tip of the city. They're driving in with blacked-out tint, so no one will know how many men came in. As for the nosy Feds, they'll see the same number of cars leaving that came in."

Sledge chuckles to himself while nodding. "Pretty fucking brilliant. Can't help but love your mind. Herrin's gonna be proud of that passage idea."

I just smirk. Pop knows about the passage but he doesn't know where it goes. This is my place and my business. He just reaps a chunk of the rewards. Axle speaks up, drawing me out of my thoughts.

"The strip club had Feds in it today. Liza watched them. One of them paid Jasmine over three-hundred dollars in lap dances to question her. She never gave them anything but the run-around. Finally, Liza told them they'd reached the limit, and the other guy sat down and started flaunting cash, saying he hadn't gotten a dance yet. These guys are ballsy. I'll give them that. Why didn't your FBI informant warn you about them doing this shit?"

"A new set of guys were put on us and the Hell Breathers," I grumble. "My informant is having to work twice as hard to catch tips now. It'll take him a while to work his way in. I just found out this morning, since it's a little hard for him to make regular calls to me."

"Shit," Sledge growls, running a hand over his bald head. "That puts a wrinkle in our comfort."

"No shit," Dash says through a sigh.

The front door opens, and Colleen and Sarah walk in with Liza right behind them. The guys all turn and whistle, pretending as though we're not having a serious discussion. The girls never know. Can't know. Only our immediate circle has the details.

Not that the girls are stupid and haven't figured out some things. But they'll never know the full extent of our operations.

"Two familiar suits are outside, sitting on top of their car and trying to intimidate us as we walk in or out," Liza says, bringing in several pizza boxes.

Sledge tilts his head, and we share a grin.

"Should we invite in our company?" he asks, crossing his arms over his chest as he reads my mind.

"Have you lost your minds?" Colleen asks, walking over to the table in front of us and spreading out plates.

"Axle, go make sure the basement is locked," I say, my smirk matching Sledge's. "Sarah, go invite in our new guests."

She shakes her head while sighing, but goes to do as I've asked.

"Why?" Colleen asks.

"Because they need to know we're not affected by them. Otherwise, they're just going to keep getting bolder."

She drops to a chair beside Axle, looking comfortable enough. She trusts us enough to know we know what we're doing. Besides, they have no idea what's going on outside of the legitimate businesses, even though they know we're anything but legit.

"Fellas, *we have company*," Sarah says in a singsong voice, teasing the two cocky sons of bitches following behind her as she sways her hips in her very short skirt.

I stay relaxed in my chair, watching as they join us in the massive room. There are four doors in here, all of them leading to various parts of the warehouse. Some hidden, some not. Their eyes immediately glance at the other three entry points, sizing up the room like good little cops.

"Gentlemen," I say all too casually as Colleen puts a slice of pizza on my plate, "how the hell can we help you? You boys seem mighty interested in my businesses."

As long as we all show them how relaxed we are in their presence, they'll start sweating. It'll put them on edge, and they'll lose that smug sense of superiority they have right now.

"Drex Caine, I presume?" the douche on the right asks.

"Apparently you guys are a little more interested in me than I am you, considering I have no idea what your names are."

They both shift uncomfortably as I slowly break through the wall of confidence they thought to be impenetrable. Then I feel someone behind me, and I tense. How the fuck did I forget?

"Well, hello," Sarah says, grinning wickedly at the girl behind me, who came down at the exact time I told her. Only she won't look as calm and collected as the rest of us. She'll draw attention to herself and this situation we never should have agreed to.

"Hi," Eve says uncomfortably, her voice almost too quiet to be a whisper.

Both feds look at her, and then they exchange a look of intrigue. Shit.

"Come here, baby," I say smoothly, scooting my chair back for her to join me on my lap. It'll go better if they think she's my girl instead of my toy. The VP's old lady has to be the most loyal to the club—or so they'll think.

Chapter 12

EVE

I'm so damn nervous, and everyone in here is looking at me. The two men in suits are showing far too much interest in me. And Drex is talking a little too sweet.

I sit down on his lap when he motions for me to do so, but I feel too on display to get comfortable. Sledge eyes Drex, whose face I can't see, and I feel like I'm stuck in the middle of a private conversation.

"I'm afraid I don't know your name," one of the guys in a suit says.

"Don't make it too easy on them, baby," Drex says while running a hand down my back, settling it on my hip as I shift in his lap.

His grip tightens, and he tugs me backward a little. To sit the way he wants me to, I'm forced to throw an arm around his shoulders and angle my body.

I don't speak a word to the two men who don't belong in here. They have to be cops. But why would Drex let them in?

"What's the matter, boys?" Sledge drawls, looking at the men with a taunting gaze, even though his expression was drastically different when he exchanged a look with Drex. "Not used to seeing a pretty girl in someone's lap? I heard you boys paid a lot of money for that. Jealous he's getting it for free?"

I swallow hard when I start feeling like a science project everyone wants to study.

Drex's lips on my neck startle me slightly, but I don't react as though I'm surprised. A devil like him shouldn't have lips so soft. It's actually another reason for me to hate him.

When he nips at my ear, I almost moan, inwardly cursing myself for my body's response to his touch. "You need to relax right now," he whispers, making sure to escape the ears of the men on the far end of the table from us. "Pretend as though this is a common thing between you and me."

I don't answer, but I do—by some miracle—manage to relax. When I turn my head, our lips brush, and his breath catches in his throat. I hate myself for wanting to feel his lips, but he's now screwed me twice and still hasn't kissed me. In my mind, I might can find a way to embrace the madness if he gives me some semblance of normalcy. And I've got to find a way to cope if I'm going to last.

If we continue on this fast-paced wild ride, I'm going to be insane by the end of the week. It'll all catch up to me at once, and I dread it.

Our eyes are locked, and everything gets intense. My skin tingles for all the wrong reasons, and the fear I need inside me is slowly fading and making way for other feelings I'm not prepared to face.

"You boys want to ask some questions, or were you just wanting to stand around and watch Drex and his old lady all night?" Sledge asks, and Drex smirks while redirecting his attention to the men in suits.

I keep my casual placement in his lap, but I manage to turn my eyes back to the men as well. Drex's hand moves up my shirt, finding the skin of my stomach, as both of the men watch.

"No questions, gentlemen?" Drex drawls, taunting them.

The one on the right finally clears his throat while Drex's hand goes higher, and my shirt creeps up just a little. When he brushes his hand on the underside of my bra, my hand on his shoulder grips tighter.

"The word around town is you're buying up numerous businesses and properties," the man says, his eyes drifting to where Drex's hand keeps getting higher.

He dips a finger into my bra, teasing my nipple, and I feel the flush on my face. This is so humiliating, but I do my best to play my part. The last thing I need is for him to be pissed at me.

"And?" Drex prompts. "Since when do the FBI care about what

businesses a person buys?"

His lips go to my neck while he plays the bored, careless man I know he's not. He's cold and calculated. Something tells me he's also a killer, considering the warning he gave me earlier.

"It always raises suspicion when someone buys up as much property as you have. Care if we take a look around?"

All the men chuckle, and the redhead snorts derisively.

Drex grins against my neck before pulling back to speak to them.

"Gentlemen, as accommodating as I'd like to be, I'm afraid I'm old-fashioned. You're more than welcome to visit the public areas of my public businesses, but I'm afraid my insurance doesn't cover anyone going where they don't belong. Unfortunately, you can only see what is right in front of you. And as you can see, this is our warehouse and hangout. Nothing special. If you want to see more, feel free to bring a warrant and I'll gladly let you have a look around."

Drex is amazingly calm, cool, and collected, even as he gropes me right in front of everyone. Fortunately it's all done under my shirt and no one can see anything but his hand moving around in there. I find myself cursing inwardly again when I have to squeeze my thighs together to stave off the ache that's forming.

"This place is a little big to be a *hangout*. Don't you think?" one agent asks.

"We also live here some. It's a place for our guys to crash when they're in town from another area. I live here a lot of the time. That's just the way we do things. Sorry to disappoint you. We're just a boring group who enjoy tinkering on cars and playing with our rides."

His lips return to my neck, and my body reflexively leans against him. "I think I'm going to take my girl upstairs now. Sarah, will show you these boys out?" Drex asks, but it doesn't sound like an actual question.

A sick, twisted part of me actually gets excited when he says those words about taking me upstairs.

I hate myself.

Drex reaches up and grabs my hair with his free hand, using it to angle my head and give himself easier access to my neck as the men walk out. One turns and looks at me, his eyes narrowing in on me as Drex makes a show of devouring my neck.

The moment they're out the door, Drex removes his hand from my shirt, stands and lifts me by my hips, and drops me on top of the table. As soon as my ass hits the hard surface, he comes to stand between my legs. He towers over me as I try to catch my breath, feeling all the more humiliated.

"Girls, I need you to leave for a minute," he says, but his eyes stay on me.

Is he going to fuck me in front of the guys? Please no. Please no. Please, please, please no.

I hear the sound of heels clicking as the girls walk away without protest, leaving me to fend for myself, but all the men stay at the table.

"They couldn't keep their eyes off her. They're going to ask questions, and then they're going to try using her to get to us," one of the men says, and I swallow hard.

"How could they use me?" I whisper, feeling so small under Drex's glower. I thought the show went well.

"They swear to you that I can't touch you if you help them catch Pop or me," Drex answers coldly, a menacing undercurrent to his tone.

What did I do wrong?

"I couldn't do that even if I wanted to. I'd never put my family at risk," I say in a near whisper again.

Drex's lips twitch, acting as though he's amused. "Good. You're scared."

Of course I'm freaking scared, you psycho.

He leans back and drops down to his chair, seeming satisfied, and leaves me on the table, feeling very on display again.

"You'd better tell me the second they approach you," he says, letting his eyes rake over my short shorts, lingering and pausing on my center as he strums his lips with his index finger in a lazy, pensive motion.

"I will. But I don't plan on leaving here. You said I'd be staying up there." I point above us, even though his apartment thingy isn't actually over this room.

His lips twitch again, and everyone at the table chuckles. I'm not sure why they find that so funny.

"Baby, you can't stay in here all the time. You'll go crazy. Besides, they'll be expecting to see you and me together some now."

I get to leave?

"Can I see my family?"

The laughter around us stops abruptly, and I feel the eyes of everyone else burning against my back while Drex's burrow into mine.

"We'll discuss that later. If you do, it'll be under supervision. You can't go anywhere without one of us with you at all times. Preferably me. But you'll go everywhere I tell you. When we're alone, we'll iron out the details. Also, I trashed your cell. I'll give you a new one, and all calls will be monitored."

Sheesh. I feel like *I'm* the criminal.

"Okay."

"Axle," Drex says, looking behind me. "Go through all her bags once more. Take her old clothes down below, and put that shit in a closet or something. It'd be too risky to toss them in the trash right now."

The guy with snake tattoos all over his arms and neck walks toward the room to do as Drex has asked. Drex is still studying me, and I'm growing increasingly uncomfortable under his unbreakable gaze.

"It's probably best if we just cut the girl loose," Sledge says, and my eyes widen in fear. There's no way I can let Benny touch me the way Drex has. I'd never be able to wash away the disgusting feel he'd leave behind.

Drex... I don't know him. It's easy to be a toy when you don't know the person. He's so much closer to my age, which again makes this easier. On some sick, twisted level, I'm even attracted to him. But I can't be Benny's.

"Can't," Drex says, his eyes still watching my every move. "Benny might think something's up. The girl stays. The feds will be going after all the women in our businesses. They'll consider them an easier in. Prepare the girls, warn them of the consequences, and call Esmerelda. Make sure she deals with anyone who needs to be fired right away."

He stands, and my breath catches in my throat as he comes to be between my legs again. Roughly, he tugs at my hair and dips my head back so that I'm forced to stare into his piercing blue eyes.

"You only get one chance. Fuck up, and you'll pay. Understand?"

My words grip the sides of my throat, refusing to leave my mouth. I'm forced to nod instead, and he leans back.

"Good. Now that you know the rules, go through the double doors and head to the den. The girls will be in there, and I'll come get you soon enough."

The first normal breath finds my lungs as he slides me off the table. He thumbs my lip while staring directly into my eyes for a minute longer. After what seems like an eternity, he finally lets me go, and I reluctantly go to join the girls who will treat me like shit. I could see it in their eyes earlier. I'm already hated; I'm sure as hell not trusted; and now I feel like the smallest infraction will get me killed. I really hope those agents don't speak to me.

When I reach the den, the three girls are lounging around, and the one he called Sarah—the blonde—smiles at me. "So Drex let you come speak with us. He was determined to keep us away from you earlier."

The redhead doesn't even try to pretend that she's less than disgusted with me. The older woman with dark hair like mine just sits, observing me with mild interest.

Very awkwardly, I sit down on the couch while the TV on the wall plays through a show I've never seen before. I don't know if I should speak, and I'm not in the mood to attempt it.

"Drex seems to be really into you," Sarah says, seeming genuinely pleased, which confuses the hell out of me.

The redhead snorts and rolls her eyes while feigning interest in what's on the screen as she retorts, "Drex had a girl sell herself to be at his beck and call. He's fascinated. It'll wear off soon. Real soon. Boredom will kill him, and he'll pass her along to one of the other guys."

Oh shit. I hadn't thought of that since he said I was his. I don't want to be passed around. I've not even made peace with being Drex's whor—um... I mean... *toy*. I'm sure as hell not ready to be anyone else's.

Sarah rolls her eyes while waving off the other girl.

"Ignore Colleen. She's just pissed because she's always wanted in Drex's bed. She's not as bitchy as she seems right now."

Crap. Just what I need. A scorned woman painting a target on my back.

Colleen scoffs, "I prefer to keep my self-respect instead of being a prostitute. Drex used to have standards."

So everyone knows that I sold myself. As if my life wasn't going to be hard enough.

"Ask questions. I know you have them," Sarah prompts.

Liza's eyes zero in on me, as if she's waiting for me to say the wrong thing. Asking questions is tricky, because I don't want to ask a question that will make someone suspicious of me—or *more* suspicious of me. The guys are probably speaking about how they'll get rid of my body if I run my mouth or help the FBI.

I don't even know what they're doing that is shady. And I don't want to know. The less I know, the safer I am.

"I really don't know what to ask," I say honestly.

Probably best to keep things as neutral as possible.

"You have to be curious about the rest of the club and us. I'm with Snake," she says, sounding proud.

Is Snake the one with the snake tattoos? That would make sense. Or did Drex call him Axle? It's all a blur.

"Snake seems quiet," I say softly, trying to add to the conversation without painting a bigger target on my back.

"Opposites attract," Colleen mutters spitefully under her breath, still pretending to give a damn about the TV.

Sarah continues as though Colleen didn't just take a stab at her. "He is. And he's incredibly sweet. Liza introduced us. She runs the strip club. I was working there, Snake saw me, Liza made a private meeting possible, and it was love at first sight. Now I work at the salon that Colleen runs. Snake obviously didn't want me stripping anymore."

Liza is still attentively studying me, and it's making me even more uncomfortable.

"Do you live here?" I ask, turning my attention back to Sarah.

"Sometimes we stay here. Usually Snake and I stay at our house. We just bought a place last month. Drex has a nice house. Will he be taking you there?"

I have no idea where I'll be going.

"Drex will be done with her before he goes back home. She'll be one of the other guy's whore by then," Colleen says, smirking as though she's enjoying the hell out of this.

Liza seems older, possibly late thirties or early forties. Her constant staring is making me more uncomfortable than Colleen taking every nasty jab she can.

"How are you ladies getting along?" Sledge asks as he comes in and sits down beside Liza. She smiles at him before he tugs her to be on his lap, and she settles down peacefully as though it's a truly normal thing.

I look behind me just as a tall guy with a large snake tattoo on the side of his neck walks in. That's not the guy I thought Snake was. Glad I guessed lucky about him being quiet.

Sarah beams up at him as he comes to pull her up from her spot on the couch. He sits down where she was, and then she ends up in his lap. He looks like a model with tattoos, almost as though he's an actor playing a part. His blonde hair, clean shave, and white teeth don't fit the dark tattoos he's wearing.

When Drex and a few others walk in, my heart tries to stop. He's drinking a beer, and his eyes are glued to mine. I can't tell if he hates me or wants me right now. I really don't want to be thrown into bed with someone else. Someone who might hurt me.

Drex seems to be about giving pleasure as much as he is about receiving it. Someone else might not care if they break my body to get what they want. I'm grateful for him, even if it does confuse the hell out of me.

"Hey," I murmur softly, looking up at him.

I need to do everything I can to not be annoying or boring. That is my new set of goals.

"Hey," he says with a lazy grin. He moves closer to me, and I stand up, unsure of what I need to do.

He tugs me to him, and I lean back when he bends to get closer to my neck.

"Get Marlene and the others over here. Drex is hogging the new girl," one guy with a deep voice says.

Drex smiles against my neck, and then he drags his lips up, letting them graze my chin and brush my lips before he pulls back.

"No one else touches her," he says, and I tremble a little.

He wraps his free arm around my back, tugging me to his body, and then he pulls his beer to his lips.

"You drink?" Sarah asks me.

I rarely drink, but that would be boring to say.

"Get her something strong. She's had a long day," Drex says, sliding his hand down to possessively rest on my ass.

My white shirt is almost see-through, and one side hangs off my shoulder. He seems very interested in that shoulder, considering his lips have moved to there. His teeth nip the flesh, and I bite back a moan as I arch closer.

"Here," Sarah says cheerily, handing me a glass of something that looks like orange juice, and I snap out of my moment.

"Screwdriver," she says, grinning when she sees me eyeing it skeptically.

I smile appreciatively and thank her, and she goes back to the couch to join the GQ model with a viper creeping up his neck. Well, a viper tattoo.

"Drink all you want," Drex says against my neck.

Then he leans back up and turns his attention to the TV before dropping to the chair and pulling me with him. If all of this has happened in one day, I dread seeing what it's going to be like in a week.

Chapter 13

DREX

"*Y*ou're drunk," I say to the girl curled up on my lap. She's smiling happily as though this day hasn't happened.

She nods lazily, wrapping both her arms around my neck before kissing it. My breath hitches, and she runs her tongue across my skin, forcing my body to tense. Why is she doing this?

"You need a minute, Drex?" Sledge asks, amused as he and Liza watch us.

I think I was speaking to them, but I can't remember what the hell I was saying when Eve's moans vibrate against my neck.

Liza doesn't trust the girl in my lap. At all. Her devout loyalty to the club makes her question the intentions of everyone.

"Nah, we're good. She's just drunk," I say casually, ignoring the fact my cock is punching my zipper, intent on getting at the sexy ass in my lap.

Colleen rolls her eyes and mutters something under her breath about prostitution and lightweight drinker. Eve really can't hold liquor. Two screwdrivers and her eyes were glossy. After three, she looks ready to pass out.

But I wanted her drunk. You learn a lot about someone when you rip the filter off.

What I wasn't expecting... "Shit," I murmur under my breath when she suddenly straddles me and starts kissing my neck harder, raking her teeth over the skin before sucking it.

I love her lips—so full, soft, and too damn inviting. I pull her closer, letting her lick her way down to my chest. The second Mack eyes her ass, my hands go to it, covering it possessively.

These damn shorts might be a little too short.

Shit. Why the hell do I care if he looks?

Her lips travel back up and she grinds herself against me. I can't fight back my groan as I pull her closer. She feels so damn good.

"Gross," Colleen growls while standing. "I'm going home before Drex fucks his whore in front of us."

"Watch the way you speak to him," Liza warns, glaring at Colleen like she's about to claw her eyes out.

I just laugh.

"She's mine, but she's no whore," I say fondly, reveling in how Colleen's temper flares to match her red hair.

Eve rewards me by only pressing closer, and Colleen leaves without a backward glance.

Deciding I should go enjoy my drunk toy, I stand, keeping her in my arms as her legs grip against my waist.

"Night, boys."

They all chuckle as I make my way out, and I allow Eve to devour every inch of my neck, ear, and jaw along the way. But when her lips reach mine, I pull back, forcing her drunken attempt to miss and hit my cheek.

"No kissing, baby," I murmur, smiling at the scowl she tries to restrain.

"Why?" she asks when I reach my room.

"Not my thing. Plus, kissing only leads to what we're already planning to do. So it's a little pointless," I say, grinning when she leans in and tries to kiss me anyhow.

I drop her to the bed, and a loud breath leaves her lips. She watches as I pull my shirt off, and her bottom lip slips between her teeth.

"Get your clothes off," I order. My fucking cock is pounding against my zipper right now, making me regret the decision to bypass boxers earlier.

"You want them off, then kiss me," she says, earning a small smile from me.

Drunk, mouthy, aggressive, and barely wearing any clothes, she looks like a fucking wet dream on my bed. She's finally making this fun. I've always enjoyed a little feistiness. She was starting to be annoying with all her compliance.

"I'm not breaking my rules. I'll fuck you, and we both know you won't try to stop me. But it's cute that you're showing some backbone."

She scowls at me without restraint this time, and I bite back a grin. I might just keep her drunk all the time. It's actually pretty damn entertaining.

"I'll be back. When I get back, be naked," I say on my way to the bathroom.

After I finish brushing my teeth and taking a piss, I walk in to find her naked. But she's also curled up in a ball and sleeping. Well, passed out is more accurate.

If it wasn't so damn cute, I'd probably be pissed. She's had a long day, so I'll let it slide.

I look at the couch and the bedding folded on top. She never did make her bed.

I guess I'll have to do it, but I need to see what I can figure out about the damn FBI agents on my ass right now.

After grabbing my laptop and the security code I'm not supposed to have, I settle in beside her and pull up the FBI database. Eve turns and puts her arm around my waist as she snuggles against me, subconsciously getting closer to me as though she's seeking security.

She looks so fragile and scared. Right now, she's holding onto me as though I make her feel safe. That's just fucked up. I'm the worst person for her to feel safe around.

Without thinking, I run my fingers through her hair, and she snuggles in even closer. After moving the laptop to the table, I lie down, and pull her into my arms for reasons unbeknownst to me. Maybe I feel sorry for her.

It's like I almost feel compelled to comfort her in her sleep. Fucking with my head. That's what this is doing.

Chapter 14

EVE

Waking up in Drex's arms is surprising, considering I thought I was supposed to sleep on the couch. What's more surprising is the way he's holding me to him, and the way I'm spiraled around him.

Ah hell. I tried kissing him last night, and I'm fairly sure I begged him to kiss me. I just keep thinking I can somehow work this out in my mind if I can convince myself that it's sort of like a relationship. Albeit an unhealthy, psychotic, somewhat morbid relationship, but a relationship nonetheless.

His eyes open sleepily, and he blinks several times as he takes in our intimate embrace. Kissing isn't his thing—his words from last night. I don't get it.

"Hi," I say with my just-awake rasp, not bothering to attempt to let him go.

"You're still in my bed," he mumbles, rubbing his face with one hand while keeping the other very firmly attached to me, holding me to him.

"Sorry. I... got... drunk?" I say, but for some reason it sounds like a question.

"And passed out after you got naked," he says with an amused grin now forming.

All he has on are his thin boxers that he must have put on after I passed out. He takes my hand to slide it over the material, letting me feel his morning arousal.

"Some things were left unfinished," he says suggestively. I bite down on my lip while sliding my hand down the front of his boxers. His eyes close as he groans, and I run my hand down the hard length of his cock.

Through the numerous tattoos, I see several scars that I didn't notice yesterday.

"What's this?" I ask, leaning down as my hand comes out of his boxers to point at a scar on his side.

When his eyes pop open, he grabs my hand and puts it back where it was, and I resume my forgotten task. He feels good in my hand—hot, silky, yet so firm.

"Knives, guns, and broken bottles. All of them. Don't stop until I say so," he says in a quick breath, his eyes closing again as his head drops back down to the pillow.

Apparently he doesn't feel like discussing his numerous hidden scars right now.

All of the sudden, I'm on my back, and he's on top of me, nudging my legs apart with his knee.

"Please be wet," he murmurs against my neck, sliding his lips lower as his finger moves between my legs.

A breath hisses between his teeth when I whimper as he pushes a finger inside me. There's no doubt I woke up ready. It's like my body is staying prepared at all times around him.

His lips latch onto a nipple, and he spreads the wetness around, as though he's making sure I'm fully prepared for him. His breath is hot, but when he pulls back to blow on my nipple, the chill of it has my back arching.

I really love his mouth.

But that's all the foreplay I get, because Drex isn't a patient guy.

In less than a few seconds, he's managed to jerk his boxers down and he's inside me, stretching me and filling me to a depth only he has explored. My moan almost embarrasses me, and his smug grin forms in response.

He pushes harder and faster, pinning my hands against the mattress as he watches himself enter and exit my body. His jaw goes slack, and my core tightens just from watching him get so turned on.

However, the loud pounding on the door makes it feel as though a bucket of ice water is thrown on us.

97

Drex stills inside, muttering curses, but he doesn't pull out.

"What?" he barks, glaring at the door.

"Sorry, man, but Mark Harrison is here."

Drex tilts his head, and then he glances at the clock. His eyes widen as though he's shocked, and then he scowls down at me like I've done something wrong.

"Shit. I'll be down in just a minute," he says, pushing into me again.

His thrusts pick up a punishing rhythm, but he stops abruptly, and curses while pulling out, looking painfully erect.

"I fucking overslept. I never oversleep," he grumbles, sounding accusatory in tone.

I'm not sure if I'm supposed to apologize or not, and I'm almost embarrassed by the fact that I want to ask him to continue before he leaves, because now there's an ache between my thighs that is hurting too much to ignore.

"You'd better be ready for me when I get back. And I'm not kidding. Don't finish that without me."

A twinge of excitement fills me, and he bends and kisses my stomach, running his tongue down to my clit before licking me. My breath leaves when he does it again, teasing me with pleasure I wasn't expecting, and like the traitors they are, my hands go to his hair and pull him closer while my legs spread wider in invitation.

He tugs my clit into his mouth, growling as he sucks it harder. But he pulls back just as suddenly, muttering a few more curses, and he lets his eyes rake over me several times. "It's after seven. I never sleep past four unless we've had a rough night. I've got to get down there, but this will be continued."

I'm so screwed up in the head. I really don't want him to leave right now without finishing what we started.

Then his words register.

After seven? It's after seven in the evening? I know we stayed up well past dawn… but still.

"Sorry," I say, feeling completely teased.

He smirks while grabbing a shirt and pulling it over his head, and then he rolls his eyes.

"You slept in my bed, and now I have to go into a very important deal with a fucking hard-on; a meeting that I'm already running late for. Your ass is on the couch from now on."

When I smile, he rolls his eyes again. "You're not supposed to be enjoying this quite so much," he scolds, but his amusement is there.

That's sobering, because it's very true. I'm sick for enjoying this.

But the alternative is being miserable and then being sent back to Benny where I'll never survive.

He's gone in the next second, still buttoning and cursing his jeans on the way out. Why did he keep me in the bed with him?

Chapter 15

DREX

"Last test," Harrison says while walking around. We've already been down here since a little bit after seven. And now it's closing in on ten. Longest fucking deal ever, but he always did love chatting and drinking before getting down to business.

"Did you bring a dog?" Sledge asks. "We have some if not."

"I brought one. This one is from Customs—the best of the best. He's on loan from a friend. If the drugs can be sniffed, this one will find them."

It won't find them. I know, because there are a series of things going on. We're the only ones with the scent cover that masks the smell dogs are trained to find. And there is a constant buzzing registering on a frequency humans can't hear. The flip of one switch turns the frequency on, and the dogs grow annoyed by it. They eventually walk away because it's so distracting, but it's not so jarring that it startles them. It's perfect.

The German Shepard is turned loose and it growls as it passes all of us. One of Harrison's men holds it on a leash, and it sniffs the car.

It snarls when it hears the annoying sound we can't detect, but it keeps sniffing.

Sure enough, between the sound and scent of dead air, it walks away, feeling satisfied that it has done its job. Harrison claps as Fido runs back to the van it came out of. Once again, I've proven to him that we're the ones for the job. For some reason, he always wants to test us.

"Impressive. What's the secret?"

My guys start laughing, but I merely smirk. "If I gave you the secret, then I'd be out of business. You know where to find me when you need me. You have twelve days before the cars are pointless. I've shown you all your new storage. Dogs won't detect shit, and you can smuggle all you want for those twelve days."

He nods, smiling happily. "Then we should get going. Time is wasting. Good doing business with you, Drex. As always."

They start loading up, and we point them down the tunnels to escape the eyes of the feds. Snake climbs into the lead car, preparing to seal the tunnel's exit doors after they're gone, and the men who drove the original vehicles prepare to resurface and go out the way they came to keep from rousing suspicion.

"Feds have come and knocked twice," Sledge whispers as the cars start driving off. "I think they're very curious about the convoy that drove in."

"As soon as they're gone, I'll go outside and deal with them. I'll get Eve down and tell her to look pretty. I don't want them thinking they can use her against me. She was nervous last night. She won't be so nervous today."

Sledge frowns as Mack goes to lead the second convoy—the distraction convoy—through the garage doors. The feds hop down from the top of their car hood, and one car starts tailing the convoy leaving. They can follow them, but they'll find nothing. All the good stuff is disappearing down a hidden tunnel. We only watch them from the monitors, even though they have no clue we're watching them.

"I'm not sure it's wise to involve her in any way."

"She's a part of us until we find out what's going on with Benny. Would *you* want to send her back to Benny?" I ask, looking to see if Sledge has suddenly gone darker.

He's the biggest softie in the place.

"You think he'd do something to her?" He looks at me expectantly, and I see the worry in his eyes. Anyone else here wouldn't give a damn what happened to her. I wouldn't have yesterday morning, but after seeing the fear in her eyes... She's scared of something, and I never even took the chance to question her while she was drunk.

"I think he's already told her he would do something, but I don't

103

know what."

"So you really think she's here for the reasons she said—money stuff. Because Snake said when that dick traitor she called a father killed himself a year ago, it put them in a really tight mess. Her sister died about a year before that, but it racked up some hospital bills, along with some sort of complication her mother had with her leg."

Sister? She had a sister?

"These are questions I should have already asked," I say to myself while pinching the bridge of my nose.

These are things we need to know. What motivates a person to get desperate enough to sell herself to Benny's club without having ulterior motives like her father had? Now things make a little more sense.

"It's only been a day, Drex. People always play with a new toy the first day they have it. But I'm with you on not giving her back to Benny if he's going to keep her for himself. The girl seems comfortable with you, and Benny would break her."

The thought of Benny touching her actually makes me sick. He's a disgusting thing to smell or look at. He's also a sick creep. I refuse to think I'm a creep. Eve sure as hell doesn't mind me touching her, and she shudders in disgust at the thought of Benny.

"So you're definitely keeping her?" Sledge asks after a moment of silence, both of us staring at the large, solid door where the feds are knocking. Our monitors show us their faces since both men staring up at the camera now. Yesterday we had two feds. Today there are three—one followed the convoy.

"Yeah. I'm keeping her. If she grows to trust me, we may be able to use her against Benny. She's friends with Ben—the son. She might could get us an ass-load of information if we need it. And she'll do anything to stay far away from Benny. If I'm right. That's a big *if.*"

Sledge's lazy grin draws up. "Girl is friends with the sissy Benny has for a son? Things make a lot more sense now. And yeah, she'd prove to be very useful. In fact, maybe in a couple of weeks she could invite the kid over. Incognito, of course. We could chat, he could see she's doing well, and he might just tell us some stuff. Boy's got to be pissed at his old man for sending a pretty thing like that your way. Think about it."

I actually hadn't thought about it. His son turned to him for help for a girl he obviously cares about. And Benny sent her off with a rival club. She was meant for Pop, but now she's in my bed. That probably pisses the pussy off twice as much.

"Axle," I yell, watching him as he walks by my room on his way to the roof. He turns and looks expectantly. "Send my girl down. Tell her to look pretty."

Axle smirks and nods before disappearing into the door, and I turn back toward Sledge. "Showtime. Verse her on what to say."

A squeal forces Sledge and me to look up simultaneously, and Axle walks out of my room while laughing. I tilt my head when he grins like a fool.

"Girl was naked and waiting," he says while heading back toward the roof again.

Sledge bursts out laughing, but I get a little pissed about the fact Axle just saw her bare body. In my bed. Shit. That's my fault because I told her to be waiting.

"Lucky son of a bitch," Sledge says through a touch of laughter. "Has the girl even eaten today?"

That's a good question. I know I'm fucking starving. It was after eight this morning before we went to sleep, and it was fucking seven before I woke up. Seven!! Now that dick has stayed until ten, and all I've had is a slice of reheated pizza.

"Verse her on what to say," I repeat to Sledge while glaring at Axle's back on his way topside.

I walk over and open the door to the two very impatient FBI agents, and smirk while I block their way and their view. "You lost, boys?" I ask, lacing each word with complete disinterest.

They both look early thirties, possibly late twenties. Just what I need—two hotshots who are trying to make a name for themselves. I should have delved deeper into their identities last night before accidentally falling asleep with Eve.

"Care to explain why a known drug dealer just spent half the night here?" the cockiest one asks.

Apparently these guys think they're intimidating. But I'm curious as to how they knew who my company was.

"Care to answer why you're harassing my warehouse like two stalker bitches?"

They both snicker quietly, acting as though this is their turf. They don't have the home advantage, and they'd be wise to remember that. It wouldn't be the first time I've made feds disappear from Halo.

"I'm fairly sure this is just a friendly chat. It's convenient that you didn't answer until after Mark Harrison left."

So they really did know who was here. Someone's leaking information. But not from my crew. So who?

I glance at my watch, feigning boredom.

"I had company, and you weren't invited. If Harrison is a known drug dealer, then why are you harassing me instead of him? Oh, that's right. In order to actually do something to either of us, you'd need a warrant."

Their laughter fades, but they keep their smirks in place.

"We don't need a warrant to knock or to sit out on the street. And that's where we'll be, Caine. All day, all night—every time you look outside, we'll be here. At your clubs, salons, spas… all of it. You'll give us a reason for a warrant soon enough."

Small arms slide around my waist, and I open my arm for Eve to step in and play the part Sledge just told her to.

"Hey, Drex. You ready?" she asks, sounding a little too sexy.

Both of the men stare at her, and I almost punch the one who bites down on his bottom lip.

"Sorry, boys," I say insincerely. "I suppose you'll have to harass me later. My girl and I have plans for the night."

Eve leans into me, kissing my chest through my shirt, and I glance down to see her wearing a short pair of shorts and a shirt that hangs just off her shoulder again. Her hair is still slightly damp, and I'm pretty sure I'd love nothing more than to push her against the wall and fuck her until she screams right now.

I shut the door, and Eve takes a deep breath while moving back just barely. You'd think she just went on a stage in front of thousands of people with the way her hands are shaking.

"I think I was supposed to say more, but I froze," she says so fucking honestly, and I can't help but laugh.

"Yeah. Little bit. But it was good enough."

She relaxes a little just as Sledge walks up, covering his smile with his hand. But then his seriousness sets in. "I think it's time we deal with this. I'll call Herrin and we'll discuss getting our lawyers out here. We pay them good money for a reason. Shit's getting real," he says, and I curse silently.

"Go eat something," I tell Eve, pulling her a little closer. "I'm apparently going to be a while."

"I'm starving," she says in a quick breath, and she almost races toward the kitchen. Damn girl is so eager to please that she didn't even bother eating.

I laugh with Sledge, and can't help but feel oddly at ease with her here. I've known the girl for two days, and yet she fits pretty damn well. But then I remind myself her father fit in well, too. He fit in quickly. He was so damn nervous that we felt sorry for the bastard and assumed he was a genuine guy.

The sobering reality has me putting my guard back up.

"Let's get to work," Sledge sighs.

"Hey," I say, suddenly thinking of something. "What about that appointment with Cecil?"

I can't believe no one woke me up for that.

"He's out of town through the end of the month or possibly longer. Left this morning. Family stuff. You want me to set her up with someone else?"

Shit. "Nah. It's not a pressing matter. I don't want anyone else inking her."

Maybe the feds will quit checking her out the second she's marked by the Dealers.

Chapter 16

EVE

For a solid week, I've slept on the uncomfortable couch. I hate it.

I'm grateful, but Drex's bed is so soft and inviting. I should be thankful that he doesn't expect me to sleep in there with him, but I'm not.

This place… It's pretty damn scary. More men have been here this week. Lots and lots of tattooed, scruffy, terrifying, wild-eyed, and gravelly-spoken men.

I haven't slept better than shit since the first night when I was kept safe in Drex's arms. Every little sound wakes me up now, and shadows of the night look like figures coming to do things that will scar me for life.

I'm paranoid and freaked out every night, because he doesn't lock his door. Apparently that's him saying he doesn't trust his guys if he locks his door on them. *I* don't trust his guys.

Drex has told everyone I'm off limits, but that doesn't stop them from leering or saying things that make my stomach roil. It's only the guys who don't stay here much. They've been bringing in more and more of them, and now this place is packed.

I don't know what's going on, but I know a lawyer showed up and talked to the feds. They haven't banged on the door or harassed Drex anymore.

He still hasn't kissed me, but he has sure as hell used my body. The madness hasn't caught up with me. *Yet.* My mind is still finding ways to cope, and for at least a week, I've managed to avoid the impending nervous breakdown.

Soft lips press to the back of my neck, and I remain still on the bed with a book under me—courtesy of Sarah. "What're you reading?" Drex asks, running his hand up under the short denim skirt I have on.

"Smut," I lie, refusing to tell him I'm reading about Motorcycle clubs and the orthodox rules they usually follow. Oh, and as it turns out, human trafficking is a real thing, but it doesn't look like the Death Dealers partake in it. My situation also don't fall under the guidelines of human trafficking. "Thought I'd get some ideas on how to impress you."

He releases a sincere laugh that makes me smile against all odds. He's nothing like I thought he'd be, and as twisted as it sounds, I actually enjoy being around him. He was… unexpected—*is* unexpected—in the best possible way. I don't hate myself for what I've had to do because it makes it… okay? I'm not sure what word

I'm looking for, but I'm glad I'm not miserable.

"Well, I'm glad you want to impress me, but I prefer to be the one in control. So no reading necessary. Get ready. We're going to the club. It's Mack's birthday, and he's going to want a good time."

The way he says that gives me pause, and my whole body gets rigid. "Not with me?" I ask hopefully, feeling sick all of the sudden.

"Fuck no," he says quickly. "You're mine. I've told you this. No one else is allowed to touch you. But there will be alcohol, drugs, and lots of other men from other clubs. You'll have to stay close. Which means you might end up with a few lap dances from the girls coming to see me. Now go get ready."

Girls coming to see him... I really wish that didn't piss me off. This is *not* a real relationship. I'm supposed to be dwelling in an endless vat of self-loathing misery instead of playing house. There's no sane reason for me to feel jealous right now. But I can't help it.

Maybe I have Stockholm's Syndrome.

I don't say anything as I go to grab a bra and a different shirt. Maybe I'll make myself look good enough to keep him distracted. Or at least look good enough to force other guys to look at me—which will make Drex focus more attention on me. He's pretty damn possessive when it comes to other guys around me.

Yep. Crazy. I'm a certifiable lunatic.

"We'll be taking my bike, so no skirts or dresses."

"I've already got a dress planned out," I lie, listening to him go quiet for a long minute.

"A dress will blow up on the back of my bike, and I don't want anyone seeing your ass. So no dress."

"I can tuck it under my legs. I want to wear a dress. This is the first time I've gotten to leave since I came here. I'd like to at least look decent."

I turn in time to see his eyes narrow and his jaw tense. I *never* argue about anything he says, so he's probably caught off guard.

"Why do you want to wear a dress so badly?" he asks, slowly coming toward me as I undo my skirt and drop it to the floor.

"I just told you why. I've ridden on the back of a motorcycle while wearing a dress. I can handle it."

His grin only partially forms. "Ben doesn't drive the way I do."

A small ruffle of excitement forms because I'm twisted and love the scary side of this jerk.

"I'm sure I can handle the way you drive. So far I've managed," I say very suggestively, and his grin only grows.

"So you have." His anger seems to dissipate as mischief settles in his eyes. I'm not sure I like that look. "Fine. Wear your dress. If

114

anyone sees your ass, I'll fuck you in front of the whole club to remind them who you belong to. Make sure you're okay with public exhibitions if that dress is so damn important."

He turns and walks out, leaving that threat suspended in the air. I really don't want to be screwed in front of an audience, so I opt to pull on a pair of shorts under the dress. I can take them off when we get there.

After hurrying around to fix my hair and applying a touch of makeup, I head down the stairs to see Drex smirking at me. He tilts his head, acting as though he's amused by the fact I went with the dress.

His black shirt hugs him tightly, and despite the heat, he has on his Death Dealers cut that has *Vice President* embroidered under *D. Caine*. His dark jeans hang low, but they fit him perfectly, which in turn might elicit a small tremble from me.

His almost-black hair is spiked up a little now—just the way I like it. And his blue eyes pop against all the dark accents. He'd be beautiful to the untrained eye, but I should know better. *Should* being the operative word, because I still find him almost irresistible even though he's nothing but death's promise to me.

He watches me while I walk all the way to him, and I bite back a grin as he eyes the white dress that flares just slightly at the hips, fitting loose enough to hide the thin, white shorts I'm wearing without showing lines.

It's as though he can't stop himself from reaching out and pulling me to him, and his hands run down my ass.

"Shorts are on underneath," I say as he slowly works the hem up.

His right eyebrow cocks up and he raises the dress up to take a look for himself.

"I'll take them off when we get there," I tell him quietly.

He leans down to my ear just as several more people start joining us. "I may still fuck you in the club, because I really like the dress."

He runs his hands run over the tops of my shoulders, feeling the skin the strapless dress has left bare. I try not to shiver, but I fail, and his smirk only grows. His thumb grazes my lower lip, and he puts his mouth dangerously close to mine.

"I'm starting to think you like me," he murmurs, staring at my lips like he's seconds away from kissing me and putting me out of my misery.

I decide speaking is stupid. He could freak out if he finds out that I'm sick enough to like someone I should hate. He might also be one of those guys who doesn't want to be liked, and he might get rid of me.

"You ready?" Snake asks as Sarah sidles up next to him. His arm drops around her shoulders, and Drex nods.

Drex's hand slides down until he cups and squeezes my ass, and then he pulls out a helmet that is sure to ruin my hair. When he tosses a long leg of his over the bike, I can't help but watch, entranced.

He's everything bad for me rolled into one hard-to-ignore body, presenting himself in the sexiest package the devil could create. I'm nothing but a weak girl falling for the man that could be my sealed fate.

When he reaches out his hand for me, I take it and lift my leg. He mutters a curse toward Mack who is trying to look under my dress when I throw my leg over. But the scruffy biker groans in disappointment when he realizes I've taken precautions.

A jolt of adrenaline surges through me when the thunderous sounds fill the garage almost simultaneously. The loud beast vibrates between my legs, and the rumble resonates in my chest, almost tickling me with sensations. I tighten my grip on Drex as the large metal door to the outside slowly rises in front of us.

The firm, deliciously defined lines of Drex's abs rest beneath my hands and grow tighter when we start to move. I think I actually giggle in excitement. It's hard to tell since all my sounds are being drowned out right now.

The slow crawl out of the garage is brief, because the second we hit the street, Drex kicks it into a gear I wasn't prepared for. The edges of my dress rise, promising I would have given everyone an eyeful, and I cling to him that much tighter as the rest of the crew follows close behind.

Giggling. I am giggling. Unbelievable.

Streetlights illuminate the road ahead, and all the headlights and taillights seem to show pause once they catch sight of the bikers nearing. I can almost feel Drex's smile as everyone on the street moves to the sides, letting us pass through as though we're royalty.

Apparently no one gets in the way of them. It's almost a powerful high, and for a fleeting second, I understand what it's like to be badass. But I'm only seeing it from the sidelines, because I never plan to really be like them.

This is temporary. Hopefully. He'll eventually grow tired of me, and if I'm lucky, my debt will be considered paid. Then I can go on and live a normal life with a real, healthy relationship—as long as I survive until then.

It doesn't take us long before we're pulling up at the club, and I swallow hard. It's not just a club… It's a strip club. Their strip club. Shit.

That's what he meant by lap dances and girls wanting to see him. He'll be like a king in here.

I clamber off the bike rather ungracefully as my nerves uncoil in my stomach. He hasn't left the garage this past week. He's had a lot of business. So I've not had to worry about him screwing around with other girls. But tonight... I have a feeling that's about to change.

The second I see him with another girl, the part of me that has made peace with this arrangement will be shattered, and the reality of this situation will sink in. I'll feel sick when he touches me after I've had to watch his hands all over another woman.

At least I had a week. That's more peace than I expected.

As everyone gets off their bikes, Drex undoes my helmet and then his. I pull my shorts off without letting anyone see under my dress, and Mack gives me a wink when he tries to steal a peek again.

Pervert.

Drex drops his arm over my shoulders as a big man with a tattooed, bald head opens the doors for us. I steel myself as we walk into the rowdy club that reeks of smoke, sweat, and sex.

My eyes immediately find the stage, and the first wave of nausea hits me. The song playing isn't meant for seduction, but the almost-naked girl on the stage seems to be changing the meaning of the lyrics with every twist and turn on the pole.

The girls waiting tables have on shorts that might as well be panties, and their shirts stop just under their breasts, hanging loosely like they were intentionally cut that way. Their high heels make my small heels look pathetic.

I felt so sexy until we got here.

"What do you think?" Drex asks over the music as we head toward a front set of booths that are all empty and near the stage.

I think I'm going to hate every second of this.

"I should have worn a different dress," I mutter dryly.

He laughs, though I don't know how he heard that. Damn.

"You can give me a lap dance later. That dress is going to drive me crazy," he says close to my ear, and then he lets his hot breath linger and leave a damp trail of fog on my jaw as he slowly pulls his lips down to mine.

My heartbeat speeds up, and he brushes his lips against mine just barely before pulling back. Damn tease.

He smiles as though he knows what he's done, and I roll my eyes before looking back at the stage. I don't stand a chance of keeping his attention in here.

He guides me into the rounded booth, and I sit down in the arch of it as Snake and Sarah join us. Drex leans back, his eyes on the stage as a new girl walks out. I already hate this night, and it's just getting started.

"They don't fuck these girls," Sarah says, suddenly very close to my ear, and I'm forced to jump a little by the startling close proximity. "Believe me, I know. I used to be one."

I turn to face her, and she offers me a bright smile and a shrug. That's not very comforting. Snake met her here, and now they're together. Obviously they *do* fuck these girls if they're interested enough.

"You look miserable already," Drex says, drawing my attention back to him.

It's a little hard to voice all the thoughts in my head. Fortunately, Sarah chimes in. "If it were a bunch of guys on stage stripping and fucking us with their eyes, how good would you feel?" she asks him, smirking as though she's baiting him.

That girl has ovaries of steel.

Drex frowns while glancing around. "It's a strip club. She seemed excited on the way here." His eyes turn to me. "What were you expecting it to be like?"

I feel like he wants me to tell him I'm having fun, but I don't feel like playing my role tonight.

"This is exactly what I expected. I'm sure there will be more things I'm expecting to come later. Can I go get a drink?"

He glances around at the very full club. "I'll order you something.

121

One of the girls should be coming by any second now to take our order."

The bar is just behind us, and standing a little lets me look over the back of the booth for a better view. Even the bartender is a sexy woman. He took me to his playhouse, and I was excited to come.

I'm so stupid.

"I don't know what I want," I say, shrugging as I lower back down to my seat. "Can I go talk to the bartender and ask what she thinks I should get? That's usually what I do."

I actually never order drinks, considering my twenty-first birthday is still a few months away. Until him, I had only ever had a drink or two in my life. But his lifestyle requires alcohol—lots of alcohol.

He lights up a cigarette, and I tilt my head. I've never seen him smoke, and I've never tasted it on him. "Sure. Take Sarah, though. No one will mess with her because they know who she is. They don't know you yet. Tell Beth to put it on my tab." He pulls me to him, and he puts his mouth right against my ear. "Don't even think about doing something to piss me off."

I'm not sure why he thinks I would, but I suddenly feel the tinge of fear that usually gets lost under the thick veil of false security I've had.

Instead of speaking, I kiss his neck, running my lips down to his collarbone, and I move to straddle his lap before I put my lips to his ear.

"Why would I want to piss you off?"

He thrusts up while holding me against him, and I moan lightly from the friction.

"Because it turns you on," he tells me.

He gauges me and measures me carefully, and then he slides his hands to be on my ass when I don't speak.

"Fine. Go. But hurry back. Elise is on next, and she'll be all over me if you're not here to help me run interference."

I can't help but grin, and he nudges me off his lap while cursing and saying something under his breath. Sarah slides over Snake who purposely doesn't move out of the booth. But Drex motions for me to go the other way, and Sledge evacuates the booth quickly to clear a path for me.

The other club members have all taken seats at the surrounding booths that are apparently only theirs. But within the club, there are numerous cuts on numerous men—all of whom look just as scary as the Death Dealers. For some reason, they're all looking my way.

"Why is everyone looking at me?" I ask Sarah as she loops her arm through mine and guides me toward the bar.

In her short pair of leather shorts and her slinky, red, transparent top with a red bra underneath, she looks so much more appealing. They should be looking at her.

"Because you look like you just escaped a convent, and you're the sexy nun they want to fuck. Drex will kill someone if they mess with you. Now why'd you want away from the booth? Something wrong?"

The concern in her eyes is genuine, and we get behind the crowd at the bar to wait our turn with the lone bartender. Sarah has been nothing but sweet to me, so I don't want to lie to her. I don't feel like I even have to lie.

"I don't want to see another girl in Drex's lap."

She laughs while shaking her head. "The girls only dance on them for a few seconds. Then they collect their tips and move on to the next man waving cash. Don't worry. Drex has never and will never take one home, because he's not the kind of guy who can date a stripper—even for a night. He's too controlling for all that, and if he wants attention, he demands it that second."

When I don't speak, she continues.

"I danced on him numerous times, and he never even knew my name. When Snake introduced me as his woman, Drex told me it was nice to meet me. He had no clue. These girls are faceless to him, other than Elise, and that's only because she comes to the clubhouse a lot. He can't stand her, so don't worry. Not all the guys think that way. Snake fell in love after our lap dance, but he wouldn't date me until I quit. Most of them don't share. Just remember that."

Considering I don't want to be *shared*, I see no reason to remember that point of advice.

"Beth!" Sarah yells, and the bartending beauty smiles over at her. "Two vodka and cranberries over here."

Beth nods and starts fixing them just as a body presses too close to mine. There are a few things that confuse me, and one of them is the fact that I can tell this isn't Drex without looking.

"So the new girl is off her leash?" a man drawls, his breath too close to my skin.

I look over to see Drex is staring at the stage as the girl I assume is *Elise* fucks him with her eyes, and I suck in a deep breath.

"I'm not on or off a leash," I say to the phantom behind me.

Sarah turns and her smile falls as she stares over my shoulder. "You can't question us without a lawyer. James has already told you that," she says, glaring at the guy who must be a federal agent.

"I can't ask you anything at the private garage. I can speak to you all I want in a public place. And it's not *you* I want to talk to."

She glares at him, and she reaches down for my hand. "Come on. Beth can send the drinks to the table."

125

I start to go with her, but the guy grabs my arm and puts his mouth against my ear.

"Drex will know about the five-hundred thousand dollars Benny Highland gave you unless you speak to me right now."

I want to laugh, but I don't. "Tell him," I say before shrugging out of his grip and allowing Sarah to start guiding me through the crowd.

We make it two feet before a man with a vest that says Dark Angels on it stops me in my tracks. "You look lost," he says, bringing up both of my wrists and forcing Sarah to lose her grip on me.

He eyes them as though he's looking for something, and then he smirks when he doesn't find what he apparently sought. His beard is white and black mixed together, and it touches the top of his chest in a point. It might be too dark to see the color of his eyes, but the deviant intentions are bright as day.

"And you're apparently not on long-term loan to Drex. Care to come outside with me? If you're a thrill-seeker, I can give you all the thrills—"

His words are cut off when a fist catches his jaw, and everyone in the club gets to their feet, all of them carefully gauging the situation. As the guy falls to the ground, Drex lowers his fist and glares at the man.

"Last I checked, this is my club and my girl."

His voice sounds so calm, but the tic of his jaw says otherwise. Sarah is at the booth, and Snake is on his feet with his hand behind him, acting as though he's seconds from pulling a weapon if need be.

All I wanted was a damn drink.

The guy on the ground laughs while wiping his mouth, and some of the men who are also wearing cuts that say *Dark Angels* are sitting down a little calmer than they stood up. The girl dancing on the stage has become a forgotten figure amongst the madness, and all eyes are on Drex.

"The girl isn't inked. Didn't realize you had a special attachment to her. My apologies."

Drex rolls his shoulders back before cracking his neck to the side. "Cecil is out of town. He'll be back soon. Now you know."

The guy nods, still laughing as he hauls himself to his feet. Then he walks back toward his table. Drex turns his glare on me, and I feel as though I shrink two feet under his glower. But his eyes move to be over my shoulder as the abandoned agent apparently nears.

"I'm not answering any questions tonight," Drex says while putting his arm around me.

"You don't have to. I just saw you punch a guy in the face. I can arrest you for that."

Drex laughs, and so does the majority of the club who are all standing once again. The agent's partner starts walking up from the back, readying himself for anything.

"You can't arrest the bloke if I don't press charges," the man Drex hit says, laughing as though the notion is preposterous. "I messed with his old lady. I deserved the kiss on the cheek he gave me. And that's what it was. A sweet little kiss."

I really don't understand this world.

Drex stifles a grin as everyone in there starts making kissing noises, taunting the agent whose jaw is tense and almost shaking. He's pissed.

"Fine. But this is a public place. I'll stick around."

"Actually," Liza says, showing up out of nowhere. "This is a private business that I run. And I can refuse to serve anyone. You boys are causing problems in my club, so you should go. Now."

He starts to speak, but when all of the bikers take a step closer, both agents exchange a clear look of defeat. I'm not as well versed on the law as them, but if Liza is telling the truth, then they really don't have a choice.

Apparently they either get scared or decide it's not worth it, because they both leave, and I blow out a relieved breath when I see Drex's anger has completely disappeared from his face.

"I think that's the first time I've ever hit someone in here," he muses, acting as though he's really thinking that over.

"It's not the first time you've threatened someone," Liza chides, walking by him on her way to our booth.

Drex shrugs and drops his arm around my shoulders. "We're getting you inked as soon as Cecil gets back. I'd rather not have to punch anyone else," he says, and I almost stumble over my own feet.

"Inked? As in tattooed?"

He just grins as though he enjoys seeing me completely horrified.

"Yeah," he says, moving his hand down to my hand, lifting it up and sucking one of my fingers into his mouth. An instant ache forms between my legs as he winks at me, releasing my finger from his teasing mouth. "You hang with us on a regular basis, then you get inked. It's the way of the world, baby, and you're mine. Everyone else needs to know it."

Why didn't that book explain this part? Most of the girls only get a tattoo when they've been with a guy for a while, but it's to please him. It's not a mandatory thing.

"I like seeing your skin, and apparently everyone else is enjoying it, too," he says while bending to kiss my shoulders. He picks me up by the waist, leaving my feet dangling, and he carries me back to the booth while he roughly kisses my neck and shoulder on my right side. It's too distracting for me to think anymore.

129

When we reach the others, Sledge moves out, bringing Liza with him, and we slide into the curve of the booth once again. Drex pulls me onto his lap, forcing me to straddle him, and in a moment of pure bravery, I surprise him before he can stop me.

The second my lips find his soft, yet firm mouth, he stills. But I don't stop. I kiss him while he's stunned, and I move my lips as though he's kissing me back instead of remaining completely rigid beneath me.

When he parts his lips—probably to tell me to stop—I push my tongue inside, and he groans before grabbing my hips and jerking me to him. When he kisses me back, everything around me crumbles into nothing, and I fall prey to him all over again.

His demanding tongue meets mine, and he tugs my bottom lip between his teeth as he pulls back. But he returns to the kiss hungrily, almost as though he can't stop himself, and my fingers tangle in his hair as I take all he'll give, because I might not get this chance again.

Chapter 17

DREX

The damn girl has surprised the fuck out of me. She tastes too good to stop. Her lips are fucking perfect—just like I knew they would be. And I'm so damn hard that it hurts.

I was joking about fucking her in the club, but now...

I pull back, doing all I can to catch my breath, and she pulls a hand up to her swollen lips. I'm not sure a kiss is supposed to be that powerful, and it's starting to piss me off that I seem to keep losing my control around her.

"Turn around," I say, nodding in the direction of the stage, and then I shoot Snake a look of warning that has him snickering before he averts his eyes.

Sledge doesn't need the warning. He most likely saw that kiss, and he knows damn well what I'm about to do to the girl on my lap who is getting braver by the second.

"What?" she whispers, seeming drunk, but she hasn't even had a drink.

131

First she fought me on her dress. Then she insisted she go to the bar. And now she has just taken a kiss she knew she wasn't supposed to.

"Turn around."

She frowns and starts to move off my lap. I wince when she shifts too painfully over my cock. Grabbing her hips, I lock her in place as I shake my head. "Stay on my lap."

She still looks confused, but she manages to turn around, still hurting me a little, and puts her back to me just as a new dancer comes on. I haven't noticed anyone on stage yet, because my mind has been twisted around the girl in my lap. She's fucking consuming me, and I don't know if I love it or hate it.

After putting her ankles on the cushioned booth seat, placing them either side of my hips, I make quick work with my zipper. I lift the hem of her dress to slide her underwear to the side. She stiffens, and I smirk as I trace her wet slit with the tip of my finger. When she shudders in my arms and her thighs try to close, I push against her a little harder, keeping my freed cock hidden under her dress.

She pushes against my finger, and her tight walls squeeze. That's enough to almost make me fuck up and do this too early, so I pull her backward until I have the perfect angle to replace my finger with my dick.

She tries to jerk off me at first, but I pull her down hard, and impale her before she can get away. She drops back against me, her back arched as she angles her head closer to mine. Her lips find mine even though that was the point of turning her around, and her daring tongue wreaks havoc on my control.

Her arm wraps around my neck as she pulls off some freaky, limber, acrobatic shit that only turns me on more, and I kiss her while rocking her hips against me. When she suckles my tongue, I find myself groaning into her mouth. I shouldn't be kissing her, but she feels good, tastes incredible, and damn she knows how to work that mouth.

I force her down with my hand on her back, and she grabs the edge of the table when our mouths break apart. She leans forward more, and her back dips into a new arch as she gives me room to thrust up. I don't know if anyone is looking, and I really don't give a fuck, because right now, I'm pretty sure I'd stab someone if I had to stop.

Eve works her hips in a rocking motion, pushing back as I thrust up, and my balls tighten in response. She's so damn wet and tight, and right now, she's the sexiest thing I've ever seen in my life.

Her head tosses back with abandon, and I swallow hard as I watch her find a rhythm to her rocking, her hips moving to the beat of the loud, fast music.

Best. Lap dance. Ever.

Her hands move from the table and go to my knees, using them for leverage, and she squeezes tightly while meeting me thrust for thrust. Then her body goes limp, and I silently hope that her screams are drowned out by the music.

Nirvana runs through my veins as my whole body tightens before painfully exploding inside her. She moves her hands to the table to hold herself up as my body continues to shudder against hers.

The walls of her sweet, wet pussy are still contracting, and it's almost painful to the post-orgasm sensitive flesh of my cock. But I don't want to move. Not yet.

She slowly starts to climb off me, but I hold her to me, blocking the view of my cock with the very handy material of her dress. She may have to wear dresses from now on.

She does as I silently command, and I zip myself back up before pulling her back against my front, putting my lips close to her ear.

"Go get cleaned up and come right back. Call me if you have any problems."

She nods, but then she stills over me.

"I didn't bring my phone," she says, sighing as she drops back against me again. I laugh when she lazily tries to stay on me, but I'm fairly positive this could get a little messy if she doesn't go clean up.

"I'll send Sarah with you. Hurry." I pat her ass before pressing a kiss to her neck.

She tries to turn and catch my mouth, but I escape the touch that seems to slay me. "You've already fooled me once. No more tonight."

She gives me a scowl that actually forces me to laugh, and I find myself surprised by that, too.

"It was good, so we can do it again," she grumbles, just as a waitress comes to set a glass of something light red in front of her and Sarah.

Sarah takes it, biting back a smile as she looks anywhere but at us.

I grin at the irritated girl on my lap, and I pull her to me to press a soft, noninvasive kiss to her lips. "Go to the bathroom."

She groans while getting up, and Sarah stands without being asked. Sledge and Liza slide out, giving them room to exit, and I watch Eve until she's out of sight.

"Thought I was going to have to hose you two down with ice," Liza says mildly while I take a sip of my beer. "It looked like you were seconds away from fucking."

I just smirk as I swallow my sip, remaining unaffected as Snake snickers behind his bottle. Sledge even fights off a grin as he pretends to be interested in the newest dancer on stage.

"Need a dance, Drex?" Elise asks, moving over Snake who waves her off.

I really hate Elise. Way too aggressive and desperate for my taste.

"Not tonight." Even if I wanted a dance, my dick would be protesting after what I just did.

She pouts while coming closer, putting her wedged heel on the table as she comes to straddle me. In nothing but a pair of thongs and a skimpy lace bra, she's nowhere nearly as sexy as the girl in white who just came on my dick. In my club. Right in front of everyone.

Definitely doing that again sometime.

"You don't even have to pay," she says as the stench of cigarettes and beer roll off her.

Eve's face appears at the end of the table, and her lips turn into a thin line while I deal with the girl in my lap—the wrong girl in my lap. Very deliberately, I make eye contact with Eve, watching her as I speak to the stripper who is still tugging at my shirt.

"He's down for the count," I say with a smirk, referring to the limp appendage she's grinding her hips against. "Just fucked my girl. You should go."

Elise stops and leans back, and her eyes follow mine to Eve. She rolls her eyes before moving off my lap and back across the table,

136

crawling over the top and shaking her ass to the music.

But I only notice her out of my peripheral, because my attention is focused on Eve. Her damn gravitational force seems to hold me captive, and I'm still deciding how I feel about that.

I'm not opposed to caring about her, but I'm also not sure that it's a good idea. Especially given our situation. She was paid to get into my bed. That's why she's here, even though I know she's slowly starting to actually care about me.

I strongly believe she's not here as a spy, because she never asks any questions, and she'd love nothing more than to hide in my room with me all day.

She never snoops, and I've left things out intentionally to lure her in. Nothing I've planted has interested her in the least bit, and there are hidden cameras everywhere that she hasn't found. If anything, she goes out of her way to avoid all the tidbits of information. If she's a spy, she's the worst one ever.

She's an anomaly, and I really love learning more about her. But at the same time, she's a *Marks*.

As she slides into the booth, her eyes move to the banished stripper who has started dancing on Mack and the others at the booth beside us.

"Sorry. You said hurry, so I did," Eve says under her breath, not

137

looking at me as she brings her drink to her lips.

"Glad you did," I say while leaning down to her neck, placing a kiss on it and waiting for her to shiver.

When she doesn't, I lean back and watch her as she stares vacantly at the stage. I'm fairly sure she's pissed, but I have no idea as to why. Unless it's because I wouldn't let her kiss me again.

"Something happen?" I ask her, watching as her drink pauses at her lips on its return.

She actually looks as though she's surprised by my question, and then she shakes her head. "Nothing happened. New dancer is on," she says with no emotion, and her drink finds its way to her lips as she feigns interest in the stripper.

I look over at Sarah who is rolling her eyes at me, and Snake stifles a grin while looking away. What the hell is going on?

"Care to tell me why I feel like I should apologize?" I ask, dropping my arm around her shoulders and pulling her resistant body against mine.

She's been more combative tonight than she has been all week.

"No reason. As you said, you're Drex Caine, and you'll fuck who you want whenever you want to."

What the hell does that mean?

"I'm fairly positive you wanted to fuck me too, considering you were the one who instigated that. And I didn't hear any complaints when you were coming on my dick."

Her eyes narrow on the drink, but I'm pretty sure her glower is meant for me. She's sexy when she's pissed.

"I didn't have a problem with you fucking me."

I love it when she curses. It sounds so hot coming out of that sweet mouth. In fact, I've actually considered recording it and putting it as a ringtone on my phone.

"Then what's your deal?"

She forces a tight smile and shrugs. "You're missing all the good stuff," she says, pointing to the stage, but my eyes stay on her.

She doesn't look at me again. For two solid hours, she stares at the stage and pretends as though that's what she wants to look at. And every so often, she'll smile or laugh at something Sarah leans over and says. But she ignores the hell out of me, and I don't like it. Not one fucking bit.

No one ever ignores me. And she's sure as hell not supposed to.

"I'm fucking beat," Snake says, groaning as he scrubs his face with his hands. "I'm ready to head back."

"Better make sure the fed is gone," Liza says while sipping a beer.

"He's probably waiting to pull your drunk asses over."

"He'll get slapped with a harassment charge for stalking me all night," I growl, growing increasingly pissed as Eve continues to ignore me and any conversation I'm involved in. "Besides, feds don't pull over people for DUIs. He'd have a uniform do it."

"Good luck with that," Liza tells me. "Be smart and call a cab."

"We will," Snake says, leaning back. "Well, we'll call for a ride when Drex is ready to go."

I silently count the drinks Eve has had. She's had three, and she's nursed the hell out of them, as though she's deliberately trying to stay sober. The ones here won't be as strong as the screwdrivers she had the other night. I want her drunk and honest.

The best way to do that is to get her home and drinking the real stuff instead of the watered down version.

"I'm ready now. Levi will have the SUVs outside. We'll take them and lock our bikes up in the garage here."

Eve tenses when I draw her close to my side, and I bend to kiss her neck. "Maybe you'll loosen up once I fuck you out of this bad mood."

When she shivers, an idea occurs to me. Considering I've been busy and unable to do anything besides fuck her, I've yet to learn anything about her. She gives vague answers with no detail. Tonight, all that changes.

I guess it's time to remind her who is in charge.

Chapter 18

EVE

I won't lie and say a pang of jealousy didn't hit me hard and painfully at the sight of the girl on his lap when I came back from cleaning up. After just fucking me, he had a stripper in his lap.

It. Sucked.

Drex walks out of the garage—yes, the strip club has a massive storage garage for their bikes—and puts his hand on my back, guiding me to the back of a black SUV as it rolls up beside us. A guy I haven't met cocks an eyebrow when he sees me climb in. He adjusts in the driver's seat, turning around and opening his mouth to speak, when Drex cuts him off.

"She's mine, Levi. Don't even think about it."

I'm *his* but he's not *mine*. Even though he sent the stripper away—just as Sarah said he would—it was still a reminder that I'm letting myself get too close. My twisted mind keeps thinking of this as a relationship instead of the fucked-up-ness that it is.

The guy driving gives me a surprised look, then he frowns as he watches Drex pull me into his lap.

"When'd you take on a stray?" Levi drawls, his eyes raking over me once again. "She looks a little too sweet for you."

Again, this dress felt so much sexier at the beginning of the night. By comparison to all the women inside the *club*, I really do look like I just escaped a convent.

Drex looks me over, and I pretend to be oblivious to his appraisal.

"She's definitely sweet," he says with a smirk I can feel.

I flush from head to toe, but remain silent. He's irritated that I'm being like this, but I have to keep my distance—emotionally. Physically, he can do anything he wants with my body. It's something I need to learn to separate—emotional and physical.

His lips find my shoulder as he flips my hair out of the way. Several others join us in the SUV as I lean back against Drex, enjoying the way his lips feel against my skin. His hand starts traveling up my leg, bringing some of the dress with it, and I immediately still, praying he doesn't fuck me in the car for everyone to see.

He chuckles against my skin before pressing another kiss to my shoulder, acting as though he can read my mind and knows my fears. Fortunately, it's a quick ride back to their warehouse/garage/short-term apartments, and Drex doesn't attempt to humiliate me in front of everyone.

As everyone starts climbing out, I shift off Drex's lap to do the same. Once we're out, he casually drops an arm around my shoulders as we walk in, and I try not to stumble to a halt when I see tons of new faces inside the massive living area downstairs.

It's a good thing this place is huge.

I want to ask what's going on, but I know better.

"Drex," a guy says, his beard sticking out everywhere as he walks toward us.

Why are all these guys so tall? Is there like a height requirement for bikers in this club or something?

"Jessie, what's going on?" Drex asks, his voice even as his arm around me tightens.

The tall, bearded, muscled-all-to-hell guy lets his eyes rake over me from head to toe. I almost feel a slime trail in his gaze's wake when he finally looks back at Drex.

"We have a problem. Cops raided one of our warehouses upstate. They had warrants, but they didn't find anything. We don't even know how the fuck they got them without us being tipped off first."

Drex's arm drops from me, and he curses while running a hand over his spiked hair, messing it up. There are a lot of men here, a few women, and a lot of eyes are focused this way.

"Get everyone to meet me in the office," Drex tells the guy, then he turns toward me as the muscled-up creep gives me one last wicked grin before walking away.

I shudder, but I know I don't have to worry about anything. I'm Drex's, and he's made it clear he won't be sharing me.

"Head up to my room. Don't come back down. Just wait on me to get done."

I tilt my head, studying his serious face.

"Everyone's going to be in the office, so I should be fine, shouldn't I?"

He almost seems amused by that question.

"When I told him to get everyone, I meant everyone important. So this place will be crawling with people who don't know you. Most of these guys are from different charters. Pop is probably on his way by now, and his crew will be here, too. Just stay upstairs."

I nod, suddenly feeling uneasy, but my stomach growls, which draws a frown from Drex.

"I'll send Axle up with some food. He'll be finished with this shit before I am."

He slides his hand down my back, steering me toward the stairs. I try to ignore all the curious eyes and catcalls that emerge behind us. I only catch a glimpse of Mr. Muscle staring at me as he speaks to Mack.

I hate Mack.

Drex slaps my ass, startling me, but he chuckles as he walks away. I practically sprint up to the room.

As soon as I'm inside, I breathe a little easier. Then I lock the door so I can keep breathing easier. It's obvious Drex doesn't want me in on the conversations.

It doesn't take but a few minutes before the music is blaring downstairs. I peek out the door, curious when I hear a lot of loud cheering and roaring applause.

My stomach tilts when I see some of the strippers dancing into the opening below, including *Elise,* who was straddling Drex earlier. I feel like I'm watching life go on from a bird's nest. But this isn't the life I envisioned for myself.

The men all seem happy to have the women coming in and dancing on them. Sarah is serving everyone drinks, and no one is messing with her.

I shut the door again, lock it—of course—and I lean against it while staring at the wall across from me. Drex gave me a phone, but I haven't used it yet. I don't want them hearing me talk to my mom, and it alerts them every time I make a call.

146

Or so they say.

I'd rather not risk it and draw attention to her.

Drex will probably be downstairs for a while, so it might be a good idea to go to sleep. If he wants me bad enough, he can wake me. But I have a feeling he might finish what he started with Elise, and I'd rather not be awake for that.

Ice runs through my veins as a thought crosses my mind. What if... What if he wants a threesome?

I'm going to be sick.

A knock sounds at the door, distracting me before I can vomit. I'm not experienced enough for this. Why did I think I could handle being someone's sex slave?

Expecting Axle and a tray of food I won't be able to eat, I open the door, but my eyes widen in surprise when I see the muscled meathead instead.

He's leaning against the doorframe, smirking while the devil dances in his eyes. I stumble backwards when he pushes inside the room, seeming eerily calm and composed.

He's not carrying a tray of food, that's for damn sure.

"Well, well, well. We were offered a toy from the Hell Breathers and I'm just finding out?"

I quickly put the length of the room between us, and my heart hammers in my ears when I hear the *click* of the door shutting behind him.

I swallow against the lump in my throat before shakily telling him, "I'm Drex's. Not the club's."

It's a futile declaration, because he doesn't seem the least bit deterred.

"No," he drawls. "You were given to Herrin. He gifted you to Drex. And we all share shit unless it's our old lady. You, little girl, are Drex's toy. Not his woman. He won't mind, I assure you."

He moves, and I suddenly feel my back against the wall, alerting me to the fact I've run out of room to retreat.

"He's told everyone not to touch me. I'm his, damn it! I'm not a toy."

I'm a fucking toy, and he knows it, because he smirks to silently tell me as much.

"He'll be pissed," I prattle on, not ready to go down without a fight. I can't stand the thought of someone else touching me. I won't... I won't survive this if it happens. I'll be as damaged and broken as I feared in the beginning.

"He'll get over it," the meathead says before diving toward me.

I scream, praying it can be heard over the music as I dart across the bed, hoping I reach the door before he catches me. But a strong, rough hand clamps around my ankle, jerking me back before I can make it to the other side.

I bounce to the bed, and then get dragged backward despite the fight I put up in vain. I kick wildly with my free foot, but it only connects with an impenetrable wall of muscle, forcing streaks of pain to shoot up my leg. My attempts of escape are mocked with rumbled laughter as he easily pins me down, pushing my front side firmly into the mattress.

Struggling to get away, I scream again when his hands clamp down on my hips, jerking me back even more until my knees are touching air and he's positioning himself between my legs.

"Don't! Please, don't!" The choked sob and desperation in my tone only provokes more laughter from the coldhearted son of a bitch.

He pins me with his weight when he drops down on top of me, and I hear the sickening, gut-roiling sensation of his hands moving between us, pushing his jeans down.

The smell of sweat, beer and smoke drench every breath I manage to get under his suffocating weight.

"Calm down, girl. You'll like it," he says through laughter.

Hot tears soak my face, and my voice turns into a hoarse cry when hope dims. But just as the sick fuck gets his pants down, the door bursts open, and an angry Axle storms into the room.

Oh no. Not him, too. I can't... I can't...

I start hyperventilating, but before I can go into a full-blown panic attack, Axle storms across the room, and his fist collides with the sicko's face. At least I assume it's his face.

Something wet splashes on me, as the weight on my back disappears. My lungs greedily suck in the fresh, cleaner air that isn't tainted by his stench. It almost hurts when I get too much air at once, and I cough while dropping to the floor.

It's then I realize the wet sensation I felt on my legs was blood spewing.

"You stupid little shit!" Sicko roars, but I don't look at him. I never want to see him again. "I'll have your ass for this. You don't fuck with me!"

"Get the hell out of Drex's room now! You'll be lucky if he doesn't fucking kill you for this, you stupid bastard."

I hear rustling of movements, but I still can't look up. I pull my knees to my chest, burying my head in the crook of my arm as I sob uncontrollably, buckling as reality crashes down on me hard.

I hear more talking, possibly yelling, but it all seems to muddle together, forming nothing more than distant white noise. No coherent sound creeps in until I hear the slam of the door, which forces me to jolt and snap my eyes up.

Axle is alone with me, the muscle in his jaw jumping as anger visibly vibrates through him. He stalks toward me, but I whimper and burrow farther into the side of the bed, thumping against the nightstand in the process.

He halts immediately, and a flash of pity crosses his eyes before he takes slow steps backwards. "Sorry, Eve," he says gently.

I shiver, but words don't leave my lips. There's no telling how broken my voice would sound right now.

"Look, I just want to make sure he didn't do anything. Can you stand?" he asks, his voice softer than I've ever heard it.

I shake my head, slinking back once again when he takes a step forward. He curses before running a hand through his hair, before turning his back.

He doesn't say anything else as he leaves me alone in the room, shutting the door on his way out. This time, my sobs come out louder as I fall apart.

Chapter 19

DREX

"Good news is, the feds didn't find anything," Pop says while taking a seat at the head of the table.

We've already gone over numerous possible scenarios of what would happen if they realized the vehicles were designed to conceal drugs, weapons, or what the hell ever else someone wants to store.

That's not our concern. We work in the gray area, not buying or selling drugs or weapons, not distributing them or transporting them, but giving them concealment.

I fold my hands together as the wheels turn in my head. "We must have an informant of some kind that's giving them tips. But apparently the informant doesn't know what we're doing, or they'd have known which spots in the warehouse to check. We call them hidden rooms for a reason."

Pop nods at me, as though he's already considered the same thing.

"Which means it's no one in this room."

I glance around to the fifteen people sitting at the table with us.

Rush leans up, propping his elbows up. I hate it when he's around, and it looks like he's about to be here on a more permanent basis.

"I think we should lie low for a while," Rush says. "At least until we find out who is feeding the feds info. It has to be someone low in ranks, or someone we work with in some form."

We work with too many people to narrow down that list very quickly, but the fed isn't directly in our outfit. I'd know it. I'm not dumb like Benny who trusts anyone in his inner circle based off a few loyal shows. Hell, I barely trust the ones who have been in our circle since before I was born.

I never trusted Aaron Marks. I liked him, but I didn't trust him.

"That'll take ages," Pop says on a sigh. "We can't lie low that long, because our clientele will be gone when we decide to return. Not to mention, it'll make them leery of trusting us if we just pull out when the heat strikes. We just need to snuff out our rat, and keep all our meetings much more discreet than we already do."

Rush nods, even though he doesn't seem to particularly agree. A prison term isn't on his to-do list, so obviously he's worried.

He's young—younger than me. The only reason he's managed to make our circle is because he's Sledge's unofficially adopted son, and he's been a Death Dealer since he was fourteen after running away from his foster family.

"What about your girl?" Rush asks, suddenly looking at me with an I'm-calling-you-out attitude. "She been contacting anyone?"

I really don't like the accusatory tone in his voice. He's too cocky with me, acting as though we're on the same playing field.

We're not even in the same league.

"She hasn't made the first call since she's been here. I'd know it if she had."

The music thumping outside the doors is almost muted, and it's not because they aren't blasting the speakers. It's because this room is almost soundproofed, assuring we have confidentiality in here.

"You sure?" Rush challenges, cocking an eyebrow at me in a way that has me clenching my fists.

If he wasn't Sledge's son… Ah, fuck it.

I stand and he stands at the same time, both of our chairs scraping the floor. We've never really gotten along, but he's never provoked me like this.

"This is my point," he says, gesturing toward me. "You've gotten attached to the girl, because you're standing here, ready to fight me for insinuating she might be the leak."

Pop breaks the tension with a riotous outbreak of laughter, and suddenly most of the others are joining in.

"Drex isn't attached to the damn girl," Pop says. "Even if he was attached, do you honestly think he'd let her roam freely and speak to whomever? He's had his eyes on her or his dick inside her the entire time."

His humor fades toward the end, and Rush drops back down to his chair, chastened. I don't need my pops fighting my battles for me, but apparently he knew I was about to kick Rush's ass.

Pop eyes me, letting me know he wants my temper under control. If we were alone, Rush would be a bloody mess on the floor right now.

"The point is, we have a leak somewhere. Find out where. And get your girl some ink," Pop says, surprising me. "Heard about the scuffle you had in front of the feds tonight. If you don't want people touching your shit, then you need to have it marked."

I groan while dropping my head back, but I nod instead of explaining myself.

"We'll draw up a plan of action, and I'll see to more discretion within the club here from now on," I announce, getting the main discussion back on the table.

"Fight!" The exclamation of that word manages to penetrate the almost soundproof room, because several people scream it at once.

Pop looks at me then at the rest of the table, before rolling his eyes and standing up when the chant outside the doors grows louder and louder.

"It's like a group of fucking kids. You can't leave them alone for long."

Sledge laughs at Pop's comment while standing, and I pretend not to see the way Sledge slaps Rush across the back of the head on his way by. Maybe people wouldn't act like kids if the old shits didn't treat everyone like kids.

Pop yanks open the door. I follow behind him and Sledge just in time to see Axle land a fist against Jessie's side, sending the big ape flailing to the ground.

Axle is half the bulk of Jessie; however, he's ten times as lethal. But Axle *never* fights unless he's passed the point of pissed off or someone has touched him. What the hell?

"Let's try this again," Axle growls. "Admit you're a slimy, raping motherfucker, and I might not continue to kick your ass like it's my sole purpose in life."

My blood chills in my veins. Axle has severe issues with guy's forcing themselves on girls. It's one of the many reasons he rides with me. It's why he pledged loyalty to me a long time ago, but he refuses to work directly under my father since Pop doesn't stop his guys from being a stereotype.

"Who the hell did he touch?" Sledge asks, a growl in his voice.

He looks toward Liza immediately, but she shrugs, averting her eyes from mine the second they accidentally find my gaze. That's when my pulse rattles around in my ears, and I feel heat climbing up my limbs when Liza's eyes then move toward my closed door at the top of the stairs.

I almost feel like I'm coming out of my skin as I stalk toward Jessie, who is pulling himself off the floor, calling Axle a string of names that don't even make a damn bit of sense.

Before he can charge Axle, I grab him back by the scruff of his neck, and toss him to the floor like he's a weak shit instead of a raging bull. He turns, rage seething from him, but the second his eyes reach mine, fear instantly flicks across his features.

"Who did you fucking touch?" I bark, barely keeping myself from reaching for Dash's gun beside me.

If he fucked her, I'll kill him. There's no question about it. I almost want to kill him for thinking of touching her.

"She's a fucking Marks," Jessie growls, fear replaced by anger once again as he leaps to his feet, glaring down at me since he has at least a good two inches of height on almost everyone in the room.

I snap. My fist flies and connects with his face, pummeling his cheek so hard that I feel something break under the contact. I'm not

157

sure if it's my hand or his jaw that just broke, but it doesn't stop me from landing punch after punch.

Every sound around us drowns down, and Jessie barely manages to connect a few weaker, less strategic hits on me. Either he hits like a bitch, or I'm too pissed to feel anything.

"Enough!" Pop roars, but I'll be damned if he stops me. This is my warehouse. My club. And that's my fucking girl in my fucking room.

Hands are suddenly grappling me, hauling me off Jessie as he falls to the floor. His eyes roll back in his head as he passes out. His jaw is definitely broken, but my hand is aching. It's the only pain I feel.

"We can't even have a damn meeting without you assholes acting like dumb fucks," Pop says, shaking his head as his furious gaze turns to me. "And, Drex, what the hell?" he growls.

I glare over at him, and I see Rush has a cocked eyebrow, as if to say, "I fucking told you so." But I ignore him and Pop's disappointed face.

"He touched what was mine, and you think I should just let him? I don't let people disrespect me in my own house." It's all I can do to speak. I need to go check on Eve, but I don't want anyone seeing her as my weakness.

She's not. At least, she shouldn't be.

Something about her delicate innocence seems to always make my protective instincts roar to life. And Jessie… That fucker needs to die.

"Get Jessie home," Pop says on a sigh, talking to one of his men. "And let's wrap this party up before more testosterone is flying. We'll resume this meeting at another time."

I shrug off the assholes holding me, and I walk over to Axle who is still glaring at Jessie like he wants him dead as badly as I do.

"What'd he do?" I demand.

Axle's jaw tenses before he looks at me. "I don't know. She's terrified right now, and she freaked out when I tried to talk to her. I came up to find out what she wanted to eat since the girls brought so much food, but I found him behind her, her dress raised up, and his pants down."

My stomach lurches, and he pauses, bracing himself for me to explode. Somehow I rein it in, and he continues.

"I didn't see much before I was on him, knocking him off her. She's not speaking."

Fuck!

I turn, ready to finish off Jessie, but Pop is right there, pushing me back as though he was expecting it.

"I'll handle Jessie. He's mine. You go check on the girl; make sure she's not broken."

For the first time in my life, I actually want to punch my own father. None of my guys would have tried this shit because I don't allow it. I don't tolerate that fucking shit.

Instead of trying deal with Pop while I'm still fuming, I turn around and jog toward the stairs. I take three steps at a time, hurtling myself toward the room.

The second the door opens, I hear a whimper, and my stomach sinks when I see her tear-streaked cheeks, red-rimmed eyes, and bruised arms. The need to fucking hit something almost strangles me, and I have to fight off the vibrating fury that is racing through my veins.

She's huddled in the corner, making herself as small as possible, and acting as though she can't see me. As I walk into the room and shut the door, she burrows her head against her arm, slinking back as far as she can. Another whimper escapes her, and I'm forced to swallow a lump in my throat.

I almost sprint toward her, but the second I touch her, she squeals and tries to wrench away.

"Fuck. Eve, it's me. It's Drex," I tell her, keeping my voice low, not expecting it to matter.

But it does.

The second she hears my voice, her head pops up, and those watery green eyes meet mine with so much relief. A small piece of something inside my chest breaks free, and an ache instantly forms.

Rarely ever does someone look relieved to see me, and those protective instincts are suddenly on high alert.

She throws her arms around my neck, almost knocking me backward since I'm off balance in this kneeling position.

As I stand, she practically climbs up me until her legs are firmly strapped around my waist, and she's shivering like it's subzero temperatures in here.

"I've got you," I soothe, rubbing her back.

She clings to me, digging her nails in as though she's a cat in water, and it's the only thing keeping me from going downstairs and blowing out Jessie's brains right now.

I don't give a damn who her father is, she doesn't deserve this. There's no doubt in my mind that Eve had no clue about her dad's dealings with us, just based on how terrified and unversed she is with the club.

Even if she did know, even if she was a spy sent to take us down, I still wouldn't allow something like this to happen to her. Fucking bastards.

161

"What'd he do?" I ask, wondering if I can even allow myself to hear it.

"He didn't... He tried... Axle stopped him before he could," she whispers, her voice tremulous and almost too quiet to be heard, and the words break until she can't speak any longer.

But I almost sag in relief. He didn't get to touch her.

Mentally, I remind myself to thank Axle later. Jessie should thank him too. As of right now, he's the only reason Jessie is still breathing.

"I have to get out of this. It smells like him." The disgust and brokenness of her tone has my rage once again brewing close to the surface.

She slides down my body, and I feel more anger surge through me when her eyes flick to the door, as though she's worried someone else might be in here. Her nails dig into my forearms as she presses her shaking body against me.

"I can promise no one is stupid enough to come in here."

Slowly, her eyes meet mine, and she blows out another relieved breath. Her hands are shaking so bad that she keeps dropping the hem of her dress, so I reach down and tug it over her head.

I expect that to be enough, but it's not. She immediately starts fumbling with her bra, and I reach around, undoing it with one hand to help her out.

Her appreciative gaze meets mine. Normally when she's stripping her panties down her legs, I'm hard as stone and ready to fuck. Not now. Not tonight. The fear in her eyes drowns out any sort of sexual air that might be here under usual circumstances.

I take my shirt off as she climbs into the bed, and I pull my jeans down, leaving on a pair of boxers.

I'll let her sleep with me, because no way in hell is she sleeping on the couch after that.

As soon as I'm under the covers, her bare body is tangling around mine, wrapping up in me like she can't get close enough. My arms go around her, tucking her against me, giving her the comfort she needs.

"Can I please sleep with you tonight?" she whispers, remnants of fear still shaking her tone.

I swallow thickly, feeling like the biggest son of a bitch in the world, because she feels like she has to ask. I realize I'm not exactly a good guy, but she should know by now I wouldn't let anything fucking happen to her. I sure as hell wouldn't shove her ass out of my bed after what she faced.

"You'll sleep in my bed from now on," I tell her softly, and she burrows closer against me, hugging me as though she has all the gratitude in the world for me.

This all started off with me wanting her more than I should have.

163

It started with me lying to myself, telling my stupid, fucked-up mind that I wanted to make sure Pop was safe. When in reality, she's been mine since I saw her.

After this, I should send her home. She's not made for this shit. But I'm a bastard, and I can't seem to allow myself to let her go. I just need to do a better job at making sure she's safe in my world, because I'm not letting her leave any time soon.

"Thank you," she finally says, her voice sounding stronger. She's fucking thanking me. Now I feel like a bigger bastard.

Instead of saying anything, I start tracing lazy circles on her back as she slowly grows more relaxed in my arms. But just as she's about to fall asleep, someone bangs on my door, and she stiffens so tight that I'm worried she's going to break.

"Christ, baby. Nothing is going to happen to you with me right here," I say softly, holding her a little tighter. She buries her head against my chest, and I pull the sheet up over her bare body, covering it from view before snarling at the door. "What?"

Eve jumps in my arms, and I inwardly curse. Just raising my own voice has scared her. Fuck.

"Coming in," Pop says, and my eyes widen. I don't want him seeing Eve.

Like a kid hiding a girl in my bed, I cover her up completely,

164

blocking her from view. I don't think he'd try to do something as stupid as deciding I suddenly don't get to keep her. And I can't believe that I'm considering kicking his ass if he tries.

The door opens as I sit up, leaving Eve under the sheet. I'd leave the bed completely if she wasn't clinging to me so tightly.

Pop walks in, along with Sledge. Fucking great. But what has the hairs on my neck standing up is the fact that Rush walks in behind them.

The punk's eyes dance with malice, and I swear I want to take out my murderous rage for Jessie out on him just because of that damn look.

"The fuck is this about?" I ask while also pulling the comforter up, shielding the outline of Eve's body from sight better with all the fluff.

Rush's eyes follow the movement, and a smirk appears on his lips. I really, really want to fucking hit him. But Eve is still clinging to me.

"Heard the details about what Jessie did," Pop says with a tight expression. His eyes move to the comforter, as though he's trying to see what I'm hiding.

"And?" I snap. It's not my usual tone with him, and he startles because of it. Then his eyes narrow as though he's about to lay into me.

"And I came to see if she's alright. She's Death Dealer property—"

"She's mine," I quickly remind him, daring him to say otherwise.

This feels like a barbaric dispute over actual property right now. It's ridiculous, but it is what it is. Eve walked into this knowingly. And despite the mess it has become, the end result is final: she's mine.

Her hands tighten on me, as though she's suddenly scared. She doesn't have to be. Pop knows better than to push me when I'm already pissed off.

"Fine. She's yours," he amends, his eyes narrowing on me again. "But she's still part of us. Which means no one touches her without consent. That's not how we treat our own. I'll see to it that this is never again an issue."

This isn't the conversation I was expecting, but I'm thankful. I still don't want him seeing her though. Hell no. He'll see what he gave up, and he might change his fucking mind. He's president. She's not marked. But shit's about to change.

"I'm calling Drake tomorrow."

Pop's eyebrows go up after hearing my words, and he frowns.

"Drake isn't your favorite person. You seriously gonna let him mark your girl up? He might do something just to piss you off."

Eve trembles against me, but doesn't dare to make a sound.

"He's not that stupid. Eve is still upset, and you all being in my room isn't helping out. We can talk about this later."

Before Pop can speak, Rush beats him to it, the smug tone ringing clearly. "Heard it was hard to speak to you without her. Considering you two are always locked up together."

Sledge growls something to him as Pop talks over him, drowning out the words. "Drex has completed a big deal and set up many more. It's fine if he's fucking his old lady on the side."

So it's official. She's mine on the serious level. That's a good thing for them to think, because it makes her family.

"Let's see this girl so I can personally apologize. I'd rather not speak to a lump of blankets," Pop says, and I stiffen again.

Rush turns his attention to me, ignoring his father and mine. Eve shifts, growing rigid against my side. Shit.

"Fine." My lips tighten as I pull the covers back just a little.

Eve pops up quickly, but holds the covers against her chest as she leans into me. Her hair is a mess, hiding most of her face, but I see Pop's eyes widen as though he just realized how fucking perfect she is.

Rush's lips curl in a smile that I want to punch off his face. Sledge crosses his arms over his chest, unaffected. He's seen her numerous times. Hell, he's been at the table while I fucked her.

Eve gingerly tucks a strand of hair behind her ear, revealing more of her face. Her plump lips are even plumper, thanks to all her tears, making them look like a fucking wet dream. Shit, *she* looks like a fucking wet dream all mussed up.

"Damn," Pop mutters, then cuts his eyes toward me. "No wonder you're so hell bent on keeping her locked away."

My arm goes around her shoulders, and she leans into me even more, as though she knows I'll shield her.

"Regretting your decision now, Herrin?" Rush says.

"Shut the fuck up," I snap, and then grimace when Eve gets even more rigid.

My anger only seems to goad him, but Sledge speaks to him in a low rumble again before Rush can pop off like a petulant teenager.

Rush glares at Sledge before walking out, mumbling something about priorities and pussy before his footfalls catch my ears. Stupid ass.

Here I am, trapped in the bed in my motherfucking boxers, while Eve holds herself against me.

"Done?" I ask, daring Pop to comment on Rush's question.

I've rarely ever challenged Pop. Usually I'm as loyal as a man can be. But I'd raise hell if he decided to take her back. Judging by the look in his eyes, he knows it.

A slow, lazy grin blooms across his face, and I immediately relax. However, Eve doesn't take the same comfort I do, because the girl feels like she might snap in two at any moment.

Chapter 20

EVE

This night is more traumatizing by the second. Drex, oddly enough, is the only thing keeping me together right now. My salvation is in the arms of a self-proclaimed killer.

I'm twisted.

And fucked up.

And naked in a room with men I don't want seeing me naked.

Drex relaxes as his father grins, but it's a creepy grin if you ask me.

Herrin is a nice looking guy for a man who is old enough to be my father, but I'm so freaking glad Drex wanted me instead. In fact, it makes me want to kiss him right now, because Herrin looks like a nightmare on legs.

He's just as tall and tatted as the others, but it's the unsettling way he looks at something, as though he's calculating its value—my value in this case.

His eyes... I've never seen eyes so cold. The other guy's eyes were the same—the one who asked Herrin if he regretted his decision. And I know Sledge called him *son* when he was scolding him, even though I didn't hear all of what he said because he was talking so low. Surely that can't really be his son. Sledge is the nicest guy in the club.

It half makes me wonder if Sledge and Herrin didn't somehow trade sons. I've seen Drex cast cold glares to many people, but he has a warmth to his gaze when he looks at me. It's reserved for me and me alone.

Or maybe I'm just crazy enough to hope for something like that.

The silence stretches on, and I grow all the more uncomfortable. The thick air is almost suffocating me.

Herrin's eyes hold mine, and that dirty, gross feeling invades. "You can have fun, son, but don't forget what we originally discussed."

Something about that has Drex tensing again, and I really don't like that.

"We'll talk about it later. But trust me, she had no idea. Tonight should be an indication of that. You didn't see how scared she was."

Sledge looks over at Herrin and grunts, "I'm with him. Girl is clueless about all that shit."

Clueless sounds about right. I have *no clue* what they're talking about, but I know *who* they're talking about: *me*. I just don't know why.

Herrin frowns, then he looks at Drex. "Coincidences are rare. Keep that in mind."

Normally, that would make me curious. But tonight, my head might explode. In fact, I honestly don't give a damn what they're speaking in code about. I'm sure it's another "spy" conversation.

Herrin and Drex speak for a minute longer, but I tune them out. Until Drex nudges me, acting as though I'm supposed to respond to something, though I have no idea what.

I look up to see two pairs of eyes staring expectantly—Sledge's and Herrin's. When I don't respond, Herrin apparently realizes I've not heard him.

"I said I apologize for Jessie's behavior. It won't happen again. We take care of our own."

What am I supposed to say? It's fine that the big son of a bitch tried to rape me? It's fine that you'd allow that if I wasn't Drex's girl? What the fuck happens when I'm not his girl? Because, it's not like Drex is going to keep me around forever.

The grim reality is swift and ugly. There's no way I'd survive in this group without Drex's protection. Even with it, I still almost ended up… I can't even think about it.

When I still don't speak, Herrin frowns. I really don't give a damn if I'm somehow insulting him. He's a sick, twisted son of a bitch to think a simple apology somehow makes it all better.

A knock at the door makes me jump, and Drex curses while tightening his hold on me. Sledge opens the door, and Axle steps in.

He's monstrous and scary as hell. Even without the snake tattoos that line his arms and neck, he'd be scary. A scar runs from his hairline down his face in a vertical line, barely missing the outer corner of his eye, and it curves and angles until it meets his chin, stopping just under his bottom lip.

But he saved me. He's still scary, but at least he's not a sick bastard.

His eyes scan over me briefly before he offers me a tight smile. I almost feel bad for how I reacted earlier when he tried to speak to me. But damn, I needed a second.

"Sorry to interrupt," Axle says gruffly, "but the guys downstairs are getting restless over the mess I made. Sorry."

He doesn't sound sincere in his apology. I don't know what he's talking about, but he seems more proud than apologetic.

"I'll handle it," Drex says, shifting, and my heart sinks as I cling to his arm, halting him from sliding out of the bed.

By some miracle, I manage not to lose the sheet that is hiding my very naked body.

173

His lips tighten as he looks at me, but I don't care how pathetic I appear. I refuse to be left alone right now. I really refuse to be left with any other man but him. No, he doesn't make it all better, but he's sure as hell stronger than I am in case that ape comes back for round two.

"We should get downstairs, boss," Sledge says to Herrin as he studies me. "I doubt they'll listen to anyone but you right now."

Herrin doesn't take his eyes off me.

"I just want to hear her speak. I apologized. She needs to acknowledge that."

Sledge makes a noise deep in his throat. Apparently he's the only one who understands this is a seriously screwed up situation.

I try to speak, just to appease him. *Let them win the battles so you can endure the war.*

No words come out. My lip merely trembles.

"You want to press her about this with me in the room?" Axle's tone is like an electrical charge that forces all three men to bristle. A chill spreads as he glares at Herrin in challenge.

Surprisingly, Herrin—the biggest alpha dick in the room—actually seems a little scared of Axle. Not that I blame him. Herrin is a tall man, but Axle is taller, and he's nothing but a solid sheet of muscle, even though he's not bulky.

174

I know he handled that muscled-up barbarian with little effort. Maybe Axle is even safer than Drex, considering Herrin seems to waver. But it isn't Axle's arms I want around me.

"I'll let the dust settle," Herrin says, acting as though he's no longer interested in hearing me *acknowledge* his bullshit apology.

Axle nods to Drex, who settles back down as the three men walk out together, leaving us alone. I shiver as the door shuts, and Drex wraps me up against his side, pulling me back down as he gets comfortable on the bed.

I wish the light was off. Tears are trying to leak out, and I'm fighting hard to keep them back. One thing is for sure, I have to get out of here before it costs me my life. Even if I'm breathing, I'll be dead if Drex ever decides he's done.

"Ignore Pop. You're barely a blip on his radar. He just likes feeling in control."

"And you just give him that control," I say before I can think, and I immediately wish I could suck the words back into my mouth.

To my surprise, he doesn't get pissed.

"He's my dad. And he's President," he says as though that explains everything.

Because I'm overwhelmed and suddenly finding my voice again, my need to endanger my stay in his bed persists. "Axle didn't seem to give a damn about who he was."

I don't look at him, but this time he does tense.

"Axle has my back. He knows he can cross lines that I can't. He didn't interject for you; he did it for me. I'm the one who brought Axle in. One day, he'll be my right hand man."

I don't point out the fact that Herrin seemed afraid of him. But he seems to feel the need to elaborate.

"Axle is unpredictable, or so my father thinks. He doesn't like him. Doesn't want him here. And though he won't admit it, he doesn't want to cross Axle. But I got to choose a crew. I wanted guys more my age, which is why I chose Snake, Axle, Dash, and a few others. Some of them you've met, some you haven't. I wanted guys I could trust and guys who weren't stuck in the old ways."

I just nod, not really understanding this complex life he lives.

He starts tracing imaginary lines on my body, and I battle with the internal war going on inside me. It's no longer living from day to day... It's worrying about the future.

And an eventual escape plan.

As much as I want to stay with Drex, I don't belong in this world.

Chapter 21

DREX

"Don't want no trouble," Drake says, looking up from the tattoo he's putting on a girl that barely has any more space for tattoos. "Go ahead and leave the way you just came in."

He does well not to show his surprise, but I can tell he's ready for a fight.

I'm not here to fight. This time.

"I need some ink put on my girl." Somehow, I manage to keep from grinding my teeth while forcing out the words.

This time his surprise sneaks out, but he masks it with impassivity almost a second later.

"Then make an appointment. I'm booked up for six months."

He goes back to his buzzing, and I run a hand over the scruff on my cheek.

"I need it today. Now, actually."

The sound of the buzzing stopping is abrupt, and Drake's cold

177

eyes meet mine.

"You lost the right to come in here and demand shit when you threw your fist into my face and put a ban on my place. Make an appointment. Be glad I'm even considering doing a damn thing for you."

Eve peeks out from my side, and she sucks in a breath when she sees Drake. Yeah… he's a scary motherfucker to a sheltered girl like Eve. He's tall, overly tatted, and has such light blue eyes that they almost look white.

It's freaky as shit.

Those freaky eyes land on her, and his eyebrow cocks as though he's shocked.

"She can't be your girl." The surprise in his voice only pisses me off.

Eve, however, steps closer.

"Please," she says, poking out her wrist for some weird reason. "I need that damn thing so those big bastards don't try touching me ever again."

Her voice wobbles on the end, and I see Drake's eyes go from cold to furious as his gaze snaps back to me.

"You let them put their hands on *your* girl? Fucking unbelievable."

"It's a long story. Just give her the ink, and I'll lift the ban. You can start getting Death Dealer business again."

That sure as hell has his attention.

"You mean the ban I shouldn't have gotten? Not good enough. You want me to ink her, then admit you're an arrogant ass."

"I'm an arrogant ass," I deadpan.

His lips twitch, but he rolls his eyes. "Fucking hell. Fine."

Eve pulls her arm back in, and I lean down to kiss her just beside her lips. She reaches up, slipping her arms around my neck, and she leans against me as though she's finally relaxing.

I love these shirts she keeps wearing—the ones that seem to always hang off one shoulder. And I'm about to take advantage of it.

Drake finishes up what he's working on, and I look behind me at Axle who is stifling a grin as he sits down. Yeah. This shit isn't easy. I'm doing good not to choke on the wad of pride I'm having to swallow.

Drake and I clashed two years ago over a girl. I had no idea he was fucking her. *She* was the one who came onto me. Then the asshole permanently fucked up some ink on my body as retaliation. I had to get the shit inked over so that I didn't have a motherfucking daisy that said "cocksucker" on my back.

Jackass dick.

I messed his jaw up, banned him from inking Death Dealers, and essentially had him shunned. Not that it hurt his business, considering he's the best in town, even better than Cecil.

He stands, still dealing with the Ink Queen, and Eve looks up to me.

"I've never had a tattoo. How bad will it hurt?" she asks, reminding me how fucking innocent she is.

And I'm still the bastard who can't let her go. Normally, I'd already be done with a girl. But Eve seems to be my weakness. I'm still deciding if that's good or bad.

"Not much. But you can squeeze my hand if it gets unbearable," I joke, earning a small pout from her.

I really love those damn lips of hers.

My thumb rubs over her bottom lip, and she leans into my touch. She might be innocent, but she's as tough as any Death Dealer in the club. Mentally, at least. Physically? I need to teach her some stuff. She needs to be able to protect herself in the future.

"Alright. Let's do this," Drake says, eyeing me curiously as Eve reluctantly turns away from me and goes to the chair he motions her to.

She sits down, and Drake comes over to me, leaving her in the room as he gestures with his head for me to join him. Great. He wants to talk. I knew this was all too easy.

I look at Axle, who nods in understanding, letting me know he'll keep an eye on my girl as all the curious ones in the waiting lounge glance her way.

As soon as we're in a different section far away from Eve and everyone else, Drake crosses his arms over his chest.

"Why come to me instead of Cecil?"

"He's out of town. Family shit or something. And Eve needs ink. She was attacked a few nights ago. I'd rather it didn't happen again, and we both know my name on her will stop all that shit."

His lips thin, and he groans before dropping his arms back to his sides. "The ban is lifted? Because I fucking hate Hell Breathers, and they've been coming in like crazy. It'd be nice if they had a reason to avoid my place again."

My skin prickles at the mention of their club. Why are they traveling to Drake? He's way outside of their normal perimeter.

"Why?" I ask him. "They used Michaels the last I heard."

He shrugs. "Don't know. But they ask a lot of questions about your dad. I tell them the generic shit, let them think they're learning more and more, when really they aren't learning shit."

181

My teeth clench. "And you didn't think to call me to warn me?"

Drake was once my best friend, until two years ago when a girl got in the way. Guys only seem to have problems when pussy is involved.

"I would have, *if* you hadn't been a dick to me. Now you know. Like I said, they think I'm giving them something."

What the hell is Benny after?

My eyes flick to the doorway as Eve crosses my mind. Pop is still leery of her and her intentions, finding her relationship to one traitor too coincidental. The fact she was *gifted* to us by Benny... Even I can't deny something is up. But Eve hasn't given me any reason to think it's more than just all a coincidence. She's actually making me believe in coincidences.

"So you want the usual DD on her inner wrist?" Drake asks, snapping me back to the moment.

Ahhh, so that's why she stuck out her wrist. She must have noticed the other girls sporting the DD tat.

"Nah. She's not Death Dealer property. I want something special for her."

Chapter 22

EVE

I was expecting a tattoo on my wrist, not on my shoulder. But Drex always seems oddly interested in that particular piece of skin, which is why I find clothes to wear that show it off, so I guess I shouldn't be surprised.

But how the hell long does it take to put a simple DD on there? At least it doesn't hurt as much as I thought it would. And no way am I looking. I don't want to see blood, and Drake said there would definitely be some blood. No thank you.

The stinging sensation continues, and I wince when he hovers over a sensitive area for much too long. Damn. He's really putting a lot of work into those two letters.

Drex walks up beside me, putting away his phone. He's been in a private room for a while, so I assume he didn't want anyone overhearing whatever he was saying.

He peers around, and a smile blooms across his face as he studies what Drake is doing. I don't know if I've ever seen him look so excited about something.

183

"They won't question if she's your girl anymore," Drake says, even though I still won't look at him. Looking at him might mean seeing my blood.

"Good." Drex sounds entirely too pleased, and he runs his hand up my bare leg, stopping on my thigh just where my shorts start.

His fingers toy with the flesh just under the hem of my shorts on my inner thigh, and I ignore the embarrassing shiver that wracks my body from that small, intimate touch.

He held me all night that night. Kept me in his bed. And he never once tried to touch me in a sexual way. He was... considerate. Which isn't what I expected from Drex.

He hasn't touched me like that since then, and he's been attentive... even sweet? It's been nice. It's also been blurring those lines even more. Fortunately, I'm a little tougher to break than I thought. Or maybe I'm still suppressing feelings about this entire new world I'm in until it's safe to really go crazy.

"I expect to see some of you guys soon," Drake tells him, and the buzzing stops as he starts wiping at my tattoo again. Shit, that burns.

"I'll spread the word," Drex says absently, still smiling at my arm even as he continues to torture me with his fingers on my leg.

"I take it you approve?" Drake asks, stepping back.

Drex's touch leaves me as he moves around to take Drake's spot,

184

and I glance up as his smile grows even broader.

"Perfect." His eyes lift to meet mine, and he winks at me. "What do you think?"

There'd better not be any blood. That's what I think as I turn my arm toward the mirror to see what has been put there. A small breath leaves my lips when I see what it says.

No wonder it took so long.

Just under my shoulder is a very easily read tattoo that proudly says, "Property of Drex" in some really neat font over the top of the Death Dealer grim reaper with a skull. Insulted is how I should feel. Relieved is how I actually feel.

No doubt no one else will ever touch me with that thing on. Even though I'm still worried about what happens after Drex is done with me, I'm not worried about things right now.

"It's beautiful," I say lamely.

Drake rolls his eyes. "If he had his name put on me, I wouldn't think it was so damn beautiful."

Drex glares at Drake as he walks off, but then his attention turns back to me. When his smile turns wicked, I can't help but get a little excited.

I'm warped like that now.

"Let's get out of here," he says while tugging my hand.

I stand as Drake comes over, putting a clear patch of some sort on my skin that feels cool to the touch. I don't ask questions. Drex is covered in tattoos, so I'm sure he knows how to deal with the aftercare for one.

His hand finds the small of my back as he guides me outside. Axle follows us, along with two other guys I don't really know. I also don't ask for names, especially since Herrin still acts like I'm some majorly awesome spy that is fooling everyone.

"You look sexy as hell with my name on you," Drex says. No one has ever accused him of being humble.

I smile about the claiming, like the idiot I am.

But his smile falls as his phone buzzes. He looks down, and he holds up a finger, gesturing for me to stay put, as he walks off to answer it.

Axle is left alone with me as the two other guys walk over to speak to Drake, who has come outside. I look at Axle, who is looking anywhere but at me.

In the sunlight, I notice that big scar isn't the only scar on his face. He has a smaller one that goes vertically over his lip, curling down to his chin, and two on his right eyebrow that seem to cause very thin spots where hair can't grow—they ride up into his hairline. That had to have been something massive.

He catches me staring too hard, and his eyes narrow threateningly. Immediately I clear my throat, feeling like an ass.

"I never thanked you," I say quietly.

His look softens, but he doesn't speak. Only nods.

Drex's arms wrap around my waist, tugging me back against him as his chin rests on top of my head. To the outside world, we look like a normal couple right now.

"We're going home," Drex announces. I thought that was the plan anyway.

"Home?" Axle asks in surprise.

"Yeah. Pop says he wants to cool things down for a week or two. He's moving our business dates back a few weeks. There are three cars camped outside the warehouse right now. He worries they know something, even though I don't know how they would."

I don't want to hear this. I don't need to hear this. However, Drex and Axle keep speaking in front of me as though they aren't worried about what I overhear.

"Shit," Axle grumbles, not seeming happy about any of this. "Fine. I'll see you when I see you then."

Drex talks about meeting at the club next week, while I try to figure things out. Is he sending everyone away?

Finally, he tugs me toward his bike, and I follow without protest. The second I'm behind him with my helmet on, my legs firmly clamped against him, and my arms around his tight middle, the beast beneath us roars to life.

Chapter 23

EVE

When he said we were going home, I of course assumed he meant the warehouse. Instead, we're at Drex's house. For the first time. And it's nothing like I was expecting.

It's not a huge house, but it's bigger than I thought it'd be. Much bigger. And there's a damn pool. Which in Texas, that's not too surprising, but often times the droughts restrict water supplies, so I've never figured out how that works.

We're isolated here. In fact, I only noticed a few houses within a few miles during the drive here. It's nowhere near the warehouse. It actually took us close to an hour to get here. I don't even know where *here* is exactly.

The inside is all modern, sleek, industrial, and pristine. I mean, you can't tell a bachelor lives here, because it's that spotless.

A massive TV is mounted on one wall, with an array of neatly assorted gaming systems. Several pieces of black leather furniture decorate the living space.

The kitchen is a gourmet kitchen. I don't picture Drex as the

189

cooking type, but he's in there right now, cooking something for my growling guts. And it smells so damn good.

He's also distracted. He's spent most of the time we've been here on his phone after the brief tour. There are two bedrooms, but he said I'd be in his. Which means I'll be able to sleep. Sadly, I don't feel safe without him. Yet he seems to think I'm a tough girl.

His presence gives me false bravado, because somehow, I know he's got my back.

He did something weird with some machine the second we got here. He flicked it on, but it never made a noise or did anything. But he said he didn't want to take chances of bugs in the house. Apparently it has something that jams those sorts of devices.

I feel like I'm living in an entirely different world.

Drex walks into the living room with a frown on his face.

"You need to call your mom and let her know you're good. She's been at the police station looking for you."

My stomach sinks and my heart plummets. Shit.

"Okay," I say hoarsely, pulling out the phone he gave me a while back. I've never even used it before.

I chance a glance at him to see he's studying me.

"Why don't you want to talk to her? You know by now I don't

190

want to hurt her? Why would I?"

There's a hint of an accusatory tone in there, as to say, *"What are you hiding?"* He doesn't understand.

Instead of answering the unspoken question, I take a deep breath and steel myself for the call.

She answers on the second ring with a confused, "Hello?"

"Hey, Mom. It's me. Sorry, I had to get a new number because—"

"Damn it! I've been looking everywhere for you, Eve!" she shrieks, emotion choking her words. "Do you have any idea how terrified I've been? Where the hell are you?"

I have to pull the phone back because of her volume, and I wince as Drex arches an eyebrow. I don't know if he's amused, confused, or just intrigued.

Mom is so loud, that I decide to go ahead and put it on speaker. Drex is going to ask what all she said as soon as I'm done anyway. Or one of his guys is listening to the call as I speak. It's not like I have privacy.

"I'm with a friend. I told you I was leaving town for a while. I've been—"

"Get home. Now! You have a family. Your two brothers are worried to death about you. Do you have any idea what you've put us

191

through? How selfish can you possibly be, Eve?"

Drex's jaw tenses, and my lip trembles. Somehow, I manage to keep the sting of her words from affecting my voice.

"I can't come home right now. I love you, and tell the twins I love them. But I got a job. I can't just come back. I'm trying to make some money."

She curses, which is highly unusual for her. "Eve, I have plenty of money. Apparently your father had a friend hold back money for him. He found me the day you took off, and I paid the bills. I guess your father wasn't the asshole I thought he was after all. There was enough left over that I was able to quit one of my jobs. But I still need you to help with the twins."

My father becomes the hero and I become the villain in this moment. I feel it. Benny told her dad had left her money. While I'm really the one paying the debt.

"I can't come home, Mom. I told you. I have a job—"

"I can't believe you're being this way. I have a job, too, Eve. The twins need both of us. I can't do this on my own. Find a place to work around here. Stop thinking about yourself and remember we're a team."

A tear creeps out, and Drex comes over. He stops short, running a hand through the longer strands of hair on top of his head. Then he turns around and stalks back to the kitchen.

"I can't. I'm sorry."

I sound like a broken record.

"Unbelievable. Fine. Do whatever. I never thought I'd see the day where you stopped caring about your family and only worried about yourself. Here I was thinking your father was the selfish one."

I saw that coming, yet even knowing she was going to go there doesn't stop the punch to the gut I feel. She has no idea what I've done for my family.

I just hang up. There's nothing left to say. And she doesn't call back to try and talk me into coming home or apologize for assuming the worst in me.

Drex comes back out of the kitchen with two plates in his hand, but my appetite has vanished. He sits down beside me, putting the food on the coffee table in front of us, while I quietly digest my mother's disgust.

He watches me as I pick at the food, nibbling small bites.

"I take it she had a low opinion of your father?" he asks, treating it as though it's casual conversation.

"Not anymore." I give him a forced smile, and he grunts while taking another bite of food.

193

"What'd your dad do?" he asks, still sounding casual, as if this isn't a touchy subject.

Lying isn't an option. Not that I want to lie. Not answering him is also not an option.

"He killed himself," I mumble.

Drex doesn't act surprised, meaning he already knew about this.

"And that's why she hates him?" He pauses a beat. "Or why she *did* hate him, rather," he amends.

I nod, hoping he doesn't want me to elaborate.

"How close were you to him?"

A bitter laugh escapes me before I can stop it, but it dies in my throat when tears threaten to emerge.

"I was daddy's girl when I was younger. But the older I got, the less he wanted me around. He grew distant... from all of us. Especially the last few years. He was barely home."

He puts his fork down, and he studies his plate for a long minute, as though he's trying to find a way to ask a difficult question.

"Did you know he worked for us at one time?"

My entire body tenses, then suddenly, without warning, a burst of laughter comes out of me. It's hysterical, crazy laughter that is taking the place of the tears that I don't want to fall.

Drex cocks an eyebrow at me as I completely lose my dignity, unable to stop laughing. Finally, I see the seriousness in his expression, and my laughter halts abruptly, almost painfully.

"You can't be serious." I shake my head, actually feeling a lot better now that I've had my weird, cathartic release. "My father was a straight-laced, stick-up-his-ass accountant. He wasn't a biker. He drove a Fiat." He just stares, so I repeat the last part for emphasis. "*A Fiat.*"

He snorts derisively, a ghost of a smile appearing on his lips. "Never said he was a biker. And he did indeed drive that small little car everywhere. But he was our accountant for a while."

My skin prickles as a weird chill settles in my bones. My brow furrows in confusion, and I desperately try to grab ahold of any memory that might give me an answer as to if Drex is lying or not.

But why would he lie?

"No," I say softly, shaking my head absently while still mulling over dusty memories.

"Any idea how he kept his family a secret? That one is baffling me. We checked him out thoroughly before taking him on, and he lived in a one-bedroom apartment downtown. No family. No history of family in his file. Nothing."

The memory of my dad and mother separating briefly after the accident that took my sister's life floods back to me. Even after he came back home, he often stayed somewhere else, growing more distant.

My dad was a tech genius, so faking a background check would be child's play if he wanted to keep us hidden. But… No. Not possible. Can't be true.

"It's true," Drex says, worrying me that I said that aloud. "He cooked our books and handled the shady shit I won't explain, so he wasn't as straight-laced as you thought."

My veins run cold, and a new brand of betrayal singes me. How could we not have known?

"My dad… was he bullied into working for you?"

He gives me a look that borders on insulted, but it fades quickly. "No. We don't force people to work for us. That just invites trouble. Someone in a situation like that would turn to the feds the first chance they got. Your dad came to us. But I had no clue Benny knew him."

I sit back to gather my thoughts, but I give up on processing my feelings.

"Benny has known me for most of my life. Well, he knew me at a glance. I never really talked to him. I rarely saw him, but the few occasions I did, he never let on like he knew my dad outside of my relationship with Ben."

Drex picks at a piece of his food as his eyes drop.

"What kind of relationship was that?" The hard edge to his tone is subtle, but I still notice it.

Is he jealous right now?

When his jaw tics, proving he's growing impatient with my hesitation to answer, I bite back a grin. He's freaking jealous. Of Ben.

Ben would die to have this ego stroke right now.

"It was… a good one?" I say, but it sounds like a question. When his knuckles turn white from the grip he has on his fork, I decide to put him out of his misery.

"Ben was my best friend. At one time, I thought I loved him. And I did. Just not the way I thought I did. Or wanted to. We were more curious than anything when… well, when we were together. We lasted for two years before we decided we were better as friends than a couple. That was almost a year ago."

He looks up at me, still seeming pissed. I can't help but poke the bear a bit.

"I can't believe you're jealous right now."

Surprise flickers across his face for a fleeting second, but then it's replaced with that cocky look he wears so well. He loses interest in strangling the fork, letting it clank to the plate, then grabs my legs and jerks me, forcing me to fall on my back as he shifts to be in between my thighs.

He stays sitting up, slowly running his hands down my bare legs, teasing the edges of my shorts with his fingers.

"Jealous?" he asks, but I'm too busy panting for air to answer him.

How he makes the world vanish and distract me from all my problems, I don't know.

He smirks as he pulls my hand up to his lips, and I'm fairly sure I moan in response when he sucks a finger into his mouth. I know that no intelligible sound emerges when his other hand starts messing with my button.

"I'm not jealous of Ben," he says seriously, shifting so that his body is more aligned with mine.

In one swift move, he's lifting me onto his lap, grabbing a handful of jean-clad ass roughly, forcing me tight against him.

"Okay," I say breathlessly.

He grins while standing, keeping me straddling his waist, but then he lowers my feet to the ground with an abruptness that immediately has me feeling bereft. I start to ask him why he's stopping, but he turns me around, pushing me toward the window of the living room until I'm forced to put my hands up reflexively to stop myself from crashing into it.

My hands hit the warm glass, just as Drex's hot breath finds my neck. I suck in a painful shot of air just as he pushes my shorts down. They drop to my ankles, and I step out of them, even though he keeps my movements restricted with his hold.

My shirt is torn off me, and my bra is tossed aside. He does all this with one hand as though it's the easiest task in the world. I stare out at the backyard, looking over the pool, trying to catch my breath, just as he grabs the lacy underwear and jerks them down to my thighs.

A whimper escapes me, and I feel him grin as his teeth graze a spot of flesh between my neck and shoulder.

"Could Ben have you whimpering before he even really touched you?" His voice is challenging, as if daring me to tell him a lie.

But I don't lie.

"No," I whisper.

His hands run up my sides, moving up until he's cupping my breasts, and he takes my nipples, squeezing them both. My knees try to buckle, but he drops one hand to my waist, anchoring me to the spot.

"Could Ben cause your knees to give out?" His husky whisper is barely heard over my own loud breaths.

199

The more he talks, the wetter I get, and he notices, especially when his hand curves around and cups me. My back arches reflexively as I try to grind against him, needing that friction.

"Did it feel like this when Ben touched you?" he asks, smirking against my neck as he pushes one thick digit inside me. But it's not enough, and he knows it.

"Drex," I whisper, making it sound like a plea.

"What, baby?" I ignore the fact that he sounds amused while he fucks me with his finger.

"Please," I whisper again.

His hands move away from me, and I immediately feel the loss. But I don't turn around because I hear the rustle of clothes being pulled off, telling me he's about to fulfill my plea.

Hot skin finds my back, and I shiver despite his warm touch. His hands move to my hips, tugging me back, and my head falls to the side when he speaks against my ear.

"Did Ben ever make you beg for it?"

My breath catches in my throat as his finger skates over my clit, leaving it throbbing even more and desperate for touch.

"No," I finally manage to squeak out, and he shifts behind me, adjusting his height so that he has the right angle.

He pushes my panties down a little more, restricting how far I can open my legs.

It's erotic torture, because I want to spread them so much wider.

He bends me, pushing me down to an almost ninety-degree angle, but I keep my hands against the glass to brace myself.

The tip of his cock grazes my entrance, as he echoes, "No." He pushes in hard, surprising me, but holds me to keep me from slamming into the glass, as he buries himself deep inside me. "The answer is no, because he never fucking owned you the way I do."

He starts moving, setting almost a punishing rhythm, and my hands cling to the surface of the glass the best they can. One of his hands stays on my waist, keeping me anchored to him as he slaps into me from behind. His other hand curls around my hair, using it to tug my head back and force me to look at him through the reflection in the glass as he fucks me raw.

It's primal, it's hot, and it's dirty. There's no finesse. No romance. But it's so damn good.

His intense blue eyes hold my gaze, daring me to look away. But I don't. There's something exciting about the stare down, something different. Even though his motions are brutal, his eyes aren't.

The lace of my panties bites into the flesh of my thighs, reminding me I can't spread my legs any farther. It locks me like this, keeping me right where Drex wants me, and I'm happy to relinquish that small bit of power.

Something silent passes between us, though I'm not sure what. But his expression changes, and his rhythm slows just barely. My breaths come out quicker when he rubs that spot deep inside me, a spot Ben sure as hell never activated.

It's almost painful because it feels so damn good. Drex's hips continue to drive into me, and the pressure continues to build in response.

Erotic pain shoots from my toes to my thighs, before I suddenly explode. That's what it feels like: an explosion.

My eyes are forced shut as painful pleasure wracks my body, stealing my breath, destroying my ability to stand, and rocking me to the core. My head spins as I barely manage to stay conscious, and my stomach contracts just as the walls inside me quiver, feeling way too sensitive, just like the rest of my flesh.

It's the most viciously incredible orgasm I've ever felt, and it seems to set Drex off too, because his guttural groan resonates in my ears. I'm almost incoherent, unable to sense time around me as he picks me up, carrying me back to the couch.

He chuckles low in his throat as I struggle to open my eyes. Holy fucking shit. What did he do to me?

He drops to the couch, bringing me down on top of him, and I pant for air, sounding like a damn dog right now as he strokes my back. His motions are tender, exactly the opposite from the window/wall sex we just had.

I think he kisses my forehead, but I'm too overwhelmed by sensation to be sure.

"That was… um… yeah," I mumble, giving up on finding words.

He laughs lightly before his fingers start strumming through my hair. I'm not sure how long we lie this way, but it has to be at least a couple of hours, because the sun is slowly starting to fade from sight. We're both going to need showers now, but it's worth it.

I could stay like this all night, but I know he probably has more in mind.

"Can I ask you some questions?"

He doesn't respond immediately, but he doesn't tense either. Finally, he says, "Sure."

"What happened to your mother?"

I don't know if she ran off or if she's dead, because he's never spoken about her.

"You want to know this right now?" he asks, sounding somewhat amused.

I look up from my comfortable placement on his chest, and he grins down at me.

"You ruined me. I literally can't move very many things on my body, so yes. I want to talk right now."

He laughs while rolling his eyes, but I see the gentle Drex in this moment—the one no one else ever gets to see.

After a minute, his smile falls, and he blows out a breath. "She died when I was little." My heart breaks for him, but he immediately shakes his head when he sees my eyes. "Don't give me that look. I can't even remember much about her, so I'm over it. Have been for years. I don't need pity."

It's impossible not to feel sympathy. It's not pity.

I reach up, stroking the side of his jaw. His eyes dart back to mine, as though he's gauging me and my intentions. *Sheesh.* It's just a show of affection.

"What happened?" I ask, still stroking his jaw.

I lean up, propping against the couch back a little so I can see him without getting a kink in my neck. My hand lazily drifts up to his hair, and despite the gelled tips, I start working my fingers through the strands.

He relaxes under my touch as though he enjoys it, and his arms loosely wrap around my middle, holding me to him.

"She overdosed."

My ministrations pause, and I suck in a surprised breath. Something I haven't seen inside the Death Dealers club is drug use. I didn't give it much thought until now, but it's surprising there isn't any of that going on.

"We don't do business with junkies," he continues, even though the conversation seems to veer off course. "Junkies are unpredictable and can't be trusted in business. But sometimes, in our work, the ones on the sidelines end up getting messed up along the way. Mom was a casualty. She couldn't deal with the life without the help of drugs. The addiction grew until it killed her."

He says it flatly, without any emotion. It's as though he's somehow put up a stone wall around this section of his life, not allowing the memories to penetrate his emotions.

It's like Drex is an island no one can touch, even if he's right in front of you.

"I'm sorry," I say softly, resuming my strokes through his hair.

He leans into my touch, and a small, peaceful breath leaves his lips.

"What about your sister?" he asks. "Marks worked for us for a while, and I never knew he had a family. I also didn't know he had a daughter who died."

205

I'm not detached from my emotions the way he is, so the mention of Isabelle is like a knife slicing through me. My chest gets heavy, and the tears teeter on the edge. I fight hard to answer him without crying.

"I was an uh-oh child," I tell him, which causes his eyebrows to arch. Shrugging, I continue. "Mom got pregnant with me when she was sixteen. Dad was eighteen. They got married immediately, because, well, they were young and thought that's what you had to do."

It's not what he asked, but he lies under me, patiently waiting for me to elaborate. My hand slides down from his hair, and I start tracing the hard lines of his chest, moving down the flow of his golden tanned abs and back up again.

"It was rough on them. But they survived the struggle. Mom thought it made them stronger, but I think my dad just got weaker. My sister was the next uh-oh. The doctors had told my mother that it'd be almost impossible for her to get pregnant again. They were wrong. She was pregnant within two months of getting off her birth control."

I roll my eyes. "Then later she had twins. So, needless to say, she can still get pregnant despite the fact it shouldn't be possible."

He shifts, sliding his hands down my waist to start drawing his own sets of lines.

"Isabelle wasn't like me. She was wild, carefree, and didn't give a damn about what the world thought of her. She was two years younger than me. She had this ability to outshine everyone and everything when she was around."

Sighing, I lean back down, resting my head in the crook of his neck. I feel his lips on my forehead, and I snuggle into him even more. The day Isabelle died is the day I stopped smiling... until I met Drex. It's also the day I stopped looking for rainbows in a sky full of nothing but dark clouds.

"One night she got busted at a frat party. She'd wanted me to go with her, but I'd told her I had studying to do. I'll never forget how annoyed she was with me that night.

"My parents went to pick her up. I stayed at home with the twins like the good daughter I always tried to be. Mom and Dad were arguing with her about what she'd done, telling her that they'd had enough. Dad never saw the other car in his lane until it was too late. He tried to jerk out of the way, but it only caused most of the impact to hit the front corner where my mother was in the passenger seat."

I breathe him in, finding comfort in his scent, before managing to finish.

"It was quick, according to the report. Mom suffered more damage, and barely survived. She still has a limp. My dad didn't suffer any damage at all. Isabelle wasn't wearing her seatbelt, and it threw her from the back seat and out the front windshield. Oddly, she barely had a scratch on her, but her neck was broken."

He holds me tighter, and I absorb the comfort. He kisses my head again, and I thread our fingers together while staring at the connection. It feels good to talk about it without being a sobbing mess.

"So Ben started dating you around the time your sister was killed?" he asks.

"About six months before the accident—give or take. Needless to say, he had to be patient after that. It was pretty much a non-existent relationship for a while, then I struggled to find the ability to stay with him after that. I felt like I owed him for being there for me though."

"Do you feel like you have to be here with me?" he asks, sounding adorably vulnerable at the moment.

"No," I answer honestly, looking up at him, then remember what is really going on. "Well, yes, considering the circumstances, but I also want to be here."

He grunts, but doesn't say anything else as he gets lost in his own thoughts.

"Why didn't someone say something about my dad working for you sooner? I assume he did something bad, since you all think I'm so untrustworthy."

It's starting to sting that Drex doesn't trust me. I don't give a damn about the others, but I do care about what he thinks. It hasn't been that long, but it feels like it's been months.

He tenses for a second, as if he's deciding whether or not to tell me anything. Again, that sting is there, but I try to act unaffected.

"He stole from us. Close to eighty million. It would have ruined our club; that's how substantial that loss could have been. We pay our guys on the side, and they have their own civilian jobs. We also use that money to fund our other business purchases, and we were in the middle of several at the time."

He blows out a breath before continuing.

"We found out quickly the money was missing. I'd never trusted him, so I had been discreetly watching our accounts, since he had full access to them. It still amazes me that he managed to keep his family a secret, because I dug into every part of his life—or so I thought. He covered his ass really well, which lets me know he cared enough about you to keep you a secret."

That doesn't even sound like my father.

"I stole a pack of bubblegum once," I say, probably sounding random. "When he figured it out, he had me take it back and apologize to the store clerk. He said stealing was the quickest way to lose your self-respect, and that he was raising me to be better than a thief."

He purses his lips, looking down at me. "People change, Eve. My mother wasn't always an addict. Life has a way of beating all the good shit out of you sometimes."

He's right. I sure as hell never thought my dad would take his own life and leave his family with no way to take care of ourselves.

My lips press against his chest, and I peer up once more. "Did it beat all the good out of you?"

His smile quirks up, and I run my fingers along his shoulder.

"Never had any good to get beaten out," he says, sounding so honest that it hurts.

It's a lie, though. He's always careful with me, always gentle even when he's rough. He's a tall guy with more muscle than it appears, yet he's always taken care with my body. I've never even had a bruise, even though sometimes I could have sworn I would. The times he's the roughest are my favorites.

And he can't stand the thought of someone else hurting me. He's good enough, even if he can't see it. Because he's the only reason I'm still me instead of a shell of myself.

Every day, he lets me feel safer to be a little more of myself. In fact, he seems to enjoy it.

"This is pretty good," I tell him, barely stopping myself from waxing poetic nonsense aloud.

He laughs lightly, but it's a weighted sound. "Yeah," he mumbles, sounding reluctant to admit it. "It is."

I start kissing a trail down his chest, and I'm rewarded with a rumble from his chest before he takes a sharp breath. My panties are still hanging mid-thigh, forgotten.

He doesn't let me get to where I want to be, though. He's too busy pulling me up, and he starts kissing my neck as my hips slide down. Slowly, ever so slowly, he pushes me down on him, and my body stretches around him.

I moan, reveling in the feel of it all. Maybe we can spend a few weeks just getting lost in each other.

Chapter 24

EVE

For two weeks, I've been in Drex's home, and we've spent most of our time in the bed. Not that I'm complaining. Being with Drex in his home is… surprisingly nice. Easy. It's like we've found a groove, and everything is natural.

Not to mention, nothing illegal is getting done in the bedroom. At least I don't think so. It makes it less stressful and almost… normal.

We haven't even left for groceries. Apparently there's a little grocery fairy by the name of Maria who keeps his house stocked but never gets seen. I'm starting to think she's a myth.

My lips strum across a semi-long scar on his side, and he makes a low noise in his throat while continuing to trace lines on my back.

"Chicks dig scars," he says, smirking down at me.

Frowning, I shake my head. "They aren't sexy to me."

When his face falls, I immediately add, "I mean, you're still sexy, but the scars are sad."

He runs his hand through my hair lazily, while keeping one hand

212

behind his head, angling up so he can see me better.

"How so?"

I trace the scar I was kissing with my finger, while shrugging and staring at it, taking my eyes off him.

"Because it's a reminder that you live a dangerous life. It lowers your life expectancy."

A throaty laughter surprises me, and I look up to see him grinning down at me now.

"You must really like me then if you're worried about how long I'm going to live."

Rolling my eyes, I prop up on him a little better.

"Why do you do it? Why take the risks? Surely you have enough money by now to just get out, if Dad stole so much from you. I'm assuming you got it back since you're not the ones who killed him."

Thank God for that.

He shrugs, looking up at the ceiling. "What we do isn't as high-risk as the drug dealers and arms dealers. It used to be some seriously shady shit before we changed things up. I like the gray area. I'm never going to be a guy who sits at a cubicle and lives the American Dream life, Eve. It is what it is."

For two weeks, we've discussed mostly my life—every detail of it.

213

I think he's trying to trust me, which is improvement. I want to know about him without knowing everything.

"Danger excites you, though. So I think I need to keep doing what I'm doing just to keep you wet," he adds, winking at me as heat blooms across my chest.

I don't argue that first part, because I'm twisted and all, but I do wish he wasn't doing anything dangerous. Whatever that is. It's a constant reminder that this is temporary, because I'm not cut out for this life. I also haven't seen or heard about any long-term commitments between the other guys and women.

"I can think of something I'd rather you did with your mouth than kiss old scars," he says suggestively.

My lips twitch, and I start moving lower, kissing my way down his stomach. His smile falters, and his eyes grow hooded as I lick the lines of that perfect V between his hips.

But before I can work my mouth down to where he wants it, there's a loud, obnoxious banging at the front door. I squeal, he curses, and the banging persists.

"Who the fuck is it?" Drex demands, lifting me off him as he grabs his jeans and starts stabbing his legs into them.

"It's Drake. Let me in."

Drex's eyebrows go up in surprise, and I quickly dress as he walks out of the bedroom, leaving the door open. I can see the front door from here as Drex rushes to it.

I don't have time to get my bra on, so I just pull my shirt on seconds before Drex swings open the door.

"What the hell are you—"

Before he can finish that question, Drake barges in, shutting the door behind him. He glares at Drex before handing him his phone.

"My phone has been blowing up with threats all day. Hell Breathers got wind of your visit to me, probably think we're playing them or some shit. Benny and his gang of douchebags just sent me that last message a few minutes ago."

I don't know what it says, but Drex's nostrils flare as he reads it. I move into the room with them, adjusting my shorts and staying out of the way. It's not like I can't overhear everything from inside the other room anyway.

"I'll call Pop. He should know they're making threats. I'll call Axle first and tell him to meet up with us at the warehouse."

"I'm coming with. These fuckers are threatening me, so I'll definitely have something to say when this is taken care of."

Drex seems hesitant, but I'm so damn confused. What the hell is going on?

215

"Drex?" I prompt.

He walks over to me while pulling out his phone. His hand cups my chin, while his thumb slides up and down my jaw, stroking it as he starts talking to who I assume must be Axle.

"Yeah... Drake is sending you some stuff. We need to meet you at—"

His words are cut off by glass shattering and explosions thundering across the house. I hit the ground hard, the breath heaving from my lungs as black dots speckle my vision.

It takes me a second to realize Drex has just thrown me to the ground and that the explosions weren't explosions at all—it's gunfire. A lot of it.

Holes appear in the walls around us as Drex yells to Drake across the room. Drake slides a gun across the floor, and Drex grabs it, keeping me covered with his body as he lifts his head to see out the window, firing with Drake back at something.

In the movies, it all plays out so clearly. You see the bullets zipping by. People are screaming, and you can distinctly hear the loud sounds of rapid gunfire, isolating each bullet that slices through the air.

In real life, it's all a blur of motion and noise, and seconds turn into hours, each ticking by so slowly that you can taste death on the tip of your tongue. And the gunfire is just loud noise that all muddles together to create the constant roar of a storm.

Right now, Drex is cold. The care and concern in his eyes from earlier is completely gone, and he fires back at whoever is unleashing hell on us right now.

Drake does the same, but suddenly more guns are shooting, because the noise drones on, getting louder and louder.

Drake curses when he grabs his arm, dropping his gun in the process. Drex ducks down and curls his body around mine, wrapping me up completely as someone tries to turn the house into a sponge.

He reaches over and grabs a small table leg, flipping it so that it crashes beside us, and I see two grenades taped underneath. With quick, jerky movements, he tosses one to Drake, who makes even quicker work with throwing it out into the madness.

Drex cover my ears just before I feel the ground jerk beneath us, the house vibrating viciously as something thunders through the air. Dirt blows inside, filling my lungs and forcing me to cough. It was already hard to breathe before the dirt assault.

Drex is suddenly off me, and I see him launch the second grenade. He dives, but the explosion kicks back sooner than it did earlier, and it rocks the house harder, letting me know it hit closer as well.

Drex crashes into the coffee table, and limply collapses to the ground. Drake is grabbing a gun, firing it with one hand while his left arm hangs at his side, blood slowly oozing from a bullet wound near his shoulder.

Drex is exposed, lying out in the open in front of the window, so I scramble up on my hands and knees, clumsily crawling to him as Drake takes on the army on his own.

His dead weight is too heavy to move, so I do the only thing I can and turn the coffee table on its side, blocking the easy view they have. If the walls won't stop their bullets, I doubt this table will, but at least it hides him better.

I cover him with my body the way he did me, and I softly chant his name, begging him to wake up. But he's out cold. His head is trickling blood from where he hit it too hard against the table when he was thrown back.

More gunfire from a different angle kicks in, and I shiver, worrying more have joined. But no new bullets breach the house.

"Fuck yes," Drake breathes, belly-crawling toward us and wincing when he has to use his injured arm. "The Calvary has arrived."

My focus returns to Drex, but he still won't wake up.

Almost at once, the gunfire stops or my ears have been deafened. I scratch that last theory when I hear tires squeal. Only a few stray shots continue being shot, but the door is kicked in before my relief can sink in.

I scream, but it dies when I see Axle rushing over.

"Is he okay?" he asks, but I can't answer. I'm still on top of Drex, keeping him covered as though Axle is going to open fire at any second, even though I know better. My mind and body aren't exactly communicating, so I don't move or speak.

"Yeah. Just hit his head pretty hard. We need to get out of here before the cops show up. The place will need to be torched," Drake tells him.

Axle nods, but when he leans down to inspect Drex, I tighten my hold on him.

"Calm down, Eve. It's just me. I need to get him out of here. You too. Come on."

Drake tugs my arm, and I reluctantly slide off Drex, looking at his lifeless body. It hurts to see him so vulnerable when I know he'd be pissed to be seen like this.

I stay on my knees as Axle curses and bends down, lifting Drex so that he can toss him over his shoulder. I couldn't even get Drex to budge, yet he is picking him up as though it's barely straining.

"I'll get him to our doc. You need to get sewn up," Axle says, eyeing Drake's bleeding arm.

"Through and through," Drake says as he stands, acting as though that makes it all okay.

I stand too, but I try not to draw any attention to myself. Axle carries out Drex, and I try to follow, but a guy suddenly steps into my path. My eyes widen at the sight of him, because he's even taller than Drex, and he doesn't exactly look too friendly.

"You can't follow," he announces, but Drake rolls his eyes while shoving past him and dragging me along.

"She just endured that with us, and did all she could to keep him safe when he went down. Fuck off, Dash."

Dash does not *fuck off.* In fact, he does the opposite of fucking off. He gets right in front of me, halting me again as Drex is loaded up into the back of a SUV. Two guys walk into the house, one of them being Snake. He doesn't even acknowledge me.

"The hell is your problem?" Drake demands, glaring at Dash.

"She made a call to her mother. Then this shit happens. This girl is smack dab in the middle of too many fucking coincidences. Drex is going to end up dead if we keep letting her tag along, pretending as though she's not a fucking Trojan Horse."

I made that call two weeks ago.

When he grabs my arm hard enough to bruise it, I snap. My body reacts before my mind, and I bring my knee up too fast for him to

220

react. It collides with his crotch, and Dash goes down like a ton of bricks, groaning when he collapses to the ground.

My heartbeat thrums in my ears, and fear attacks my instincts, forcing me to recoil instead of running like I should. They might actually kill me now. As if this is all my fault.

"Stop dicking around and get her loaded up," Snake calls from the back.

How could he? He's seen me with Drex. He knows I'm not out to freaking hurt him!

"I'll take her with me," Drake growls.

Since he seems to be the only one to *not* want me dead, I follow without hesitation.

"The hell you will," Dash says through strain, coughing as he tries to stand. "Herrin wants her at the clubhouse. That's where we're taking her. I've already called him and told him Drex would be dead if we hadn't gotten here when we did. It's fortunate we were at Axle's house, which isn't too far away. She's a fucking menace, and we're sick of playing this game."

Axle finally speaks up. "Let Drake take her. We need to get Drex to a hospital. He's still out. It could be bad. Take care of the house, grab the shit he'll want to keep, and torch the rest."

Dash curses as I quickly climb onto the back of Drake's bike.

221

"I really hope I don't get killed for this," he groans, wincing as he hands me his only helmet. "But I'm not about to let them make you disappear."

Sickness unfurls in my stomach as bile rises. This day actually started out pretty good. But I should have known better than to think it could last.

My eyes flick to Drex as Axle shuts the door. It takes all my strength not to beg them to let me go with them, even knowing it could result in my death.

But then I remember just how little Drex trusts me. I can't stand the thought of him wanting me dead, too.

Pain slices through me as Drake revs the bike, and I clutch his middle as he drives us away. I somehow just became public enemy number one to the Death Dealers.

End of Book One. Book 2 is available now on all venues.

Please note, Book 2 is much longer and will have the conclusion for Drex and Eve. This is not a serial. It is a series, as book 3 features another main couple.

ABOUT THE AUTHOR

C.M. Owens is a USA Today Bestselling author of over 30 novels. She always loves a good laugh, and lives and breathes the emotions of the characters she becomes attached to. Though she came from a family of musicians, she has zero abilities with instruments, sounds like a strangled cat when she sings, and her dancing is downright embarrassing. Just ask anyone who knows her. Her creativity rests solely in the written word. Her family is grateful that she gave up her quest to become a famous singer.

You can find her Facebook, Twitter, and Instagram.

Instagram: @cmowensauthor

Twitter: @cmowensauthor

Facebook: facebook.com/CMOwensAuthor

There are two Facebook groups, the teaser group, and the book club where you can always find her hanging out with her fans and readers.

Printed in Great Britain
by Amazon

83187854R00139